'Well, well!' Daniel murmured softly.

'If it isn't the lady of the lake!' He grinned. 'The last time I saw the delectable-looking lady in white she was covered in pond-weed,' Daniel said, 'and she was giving me a diatribe on the use of antibiotics. I certainly never expected to see her again so soon.'

'You didn't? If you're talking about Helen Blake, you're going to be seeing her all the time, I'm afraid. She's your registrar.'

Dear Reader

It's a children and animals month this time, as we have NO SHADOW OF DOUBT from Abigail Gordon, and TO LOVE AGAIN by Laura MacDonald dealing with paediatrics, and VET IN A QUANDARY by Mary Bowring dealing mainly with small animals — very appropriate for spring! We also introduce new Australian author Mary Hawkins, who begins her medical career at the opposite end of the spectrum with a gentle look at the care of the elderly. Jean and Chris are delightful characters. Enjoy!

The Editor

Abigail Gordon began writing some years ago at the suggestion of her sister, who is herself an established writer. She has found it an absorbing and fulfilling way of expressing herself, and feels that in the medical romance there is an opportunity to present realistically strong dramatic situations with which readers can identify. Abigail lives in a Cheshire village near Stockport, is married with three grown-up sons, and currently has three grandchildren.

Recent titles by the same author:

JOEL'S WAY

NO SHADOW OF DOUBT

BY
ABIGAIL GORDON

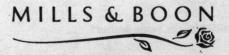

MILLS & BOON LIMITED
ETON HOUSE, 18–24 PARADISE ROAD
RICHMOND, SURREY, TW9 1SR

*First published in Great Britain 1994
by Mills & Boon Limited*

© Abigail Gordon 1994

*Australian copyright 1994
Philippine copyright 1994
This edition 1994*

ISBN 0 263 78562 9

*Set in 10 on 12 pt Linotron Times
03-9404-55733*

*Typeset in Great Britain by Centracet, Cambridge
Made and printed in Great Britain*

CHAPTER ONE

LINNIAS PARK at seven o'clock on a July morning was cool, quiet, and very green. The huge golden ball of the sun hadn't yet pushed its way through the clouds and the air was fresh and tangy.

Helen Blake jogged with a measured, easy stride along the path that encircled the lake. She loved this place in the early morning. There was a feeling of timelessness about it, as if its glittering lake had been untouched since man first walked the earth, the terraces and rose gardens wrapped in some ancient time-warp, instead of created only twenty years ago as part of a large leisure area that dominated the gracious Midlands town.

On a small rocky island in the centre of the lake wildfowl strutted around their small kingdom, early risers like herself, to a background of birdsong from the trees.

Later in the day children would play on the vast grassy slopes, and youngsters dash around the tennis courts, but at seven in the morning there was peace and she loved it.

Her two weeks' holiday was almost over, if it could be called that. She'd spent the time moving into a cottage at the far side of the park, and the early sprint that she'd embarked on that first busy morning was proving to be a very pleasurable exercise which relaxed and invigorated her. She had vowed that she was going to keep it up, however exhausted she might be, once she was back on the wards of the busy children's hospital not far from her new home. Helen intended to find out how late the park stayed open. . .treating sick children was no nine-to-five job, and so it would have to be if and when the opportunity arose.

Feet slapping rhythmically on the concrete path, she jogged along in the silence. So far on her morning runs she'd seen one other jogger and gardeners on an early shift, and today was the same, until she came out of a clump of trees and saw ahead of her two little boys leaning precariously over the water's edge.

In that first glimpse Helen was aware of small blond heads close together as they peered into the water, little brown bodies, barefoot, clad in only identical dark blue shorts. She increased her pace, anger rising inside her. There was no one else in sight, and the eldest of them didn't look any more than five years old. What on earth were they doing in the park at this hour on their own?

She made no sound as she drew near; a sudden shout might startle them and make one or both of them overbalance, and she'd no idea how deep the lake was.

'Look! There it is, Thomas,' the bigger boy called out suddenly, his voice high and excited, and a huge carp slid out of the reeds by the water's edge.

'Where? I can't see it!' the smaller one cried, and as if it were happening in slow motion Helen saw him lean forward, lose his footing, and topple slowly into the still green waters of the lake. She was so close that her fingers brushed the waistband of his trousers, but before she could get a grip on him he was gone.

'Tommy!' the other boy cried in terror. 'Help us! He's going to drown!' He struggled as Helen yanked him back from the edge, and even as she was doing so she was kicking off her trainers and struggling out of her jogging pants.

'Go and get help!' she cried. 'Quick! As fast as you can!' And as he turned and fled she stepped into the water.

At first glance it didn't look too deep, four feet at the most, but she could feel her feet sinking into the thick sludge on the bottom and weeds were tangling around her legs.

A small wet head bobbed up a few feet away and as she lunged forward to grasp him the bed of the lake shelved beneath her feet and she went under. Helen was a strong swimmer but she panicked nevertheless. The weeds seemed to be dragging her down and it seemed like an eternity before she surfaced again, but she did, and saw thankfully that the child was close by.

This time she managed to grab him and as she pulled him with her, striking out for the bank, she felt the bottom of the lake beneath her feet again and she was able to tread water until she heaved him on to the land. As she bent over him he started to cry and her heart leapt with relief. He was white-faced and covered in weeds and slime, but otherwise appeared to be all right.

Feet were pounding towards them, and when she looked up a tall, bronzed youth was racing along the side of the lake, horror written all over one of the most handsome faces she'd ever seen, and close on his heels was the other small boy.

He dropped on his knees beside the child. 'Thomas!' he cried. 'Are you all right?'

His small lips began to tremble. 'No, I'm not, Bruno. I feel sick.'

'Good,' Helen said with quick approval. 'Bend him

over and let him get on with it. It will help to get rid of any stagnant water he's swallowed.'

'Yes, ma'am,' he said meekly, and when little Thomas had finished retching he picked him up in his arms and said uncomfortably, 'Thank you for getting him out of the water. If you will come back to the house with us you can get cleaned up there.'

Helen could just imagine what she looked like. Only a quarter of an hour ago she had been immaculate in a smart jogging suit that had been a Christmas present from her mother, with her dark hair in its short stylish cut held back with a sweat-band, and expensive trainers on her feet.

She was a tall, slender girl with curves in all the right places, and a frank, open face that was made beautiful by a kind mouth and amazing hazel eyes, but at that moment, like the child in his arms, she was covered in green slime and various other components of pond life, and was angrily aware that on the face of it this man was to blame.

The house he was hurrying towards was one of the large expensive residences on the opposite side of the lake to her own. They were approaching it from the back through a wrought-iron gate set in a high brick wall, and if Helen hadn't been so annoyed she might have been impressed by its opulence.

'Are you the father of the children?' she asked coldly as she hurried along beside him.

He flushed. 'No. I am Bruno Hengist, the au pair.'

She stared at him, her outrage momentarily forgotten. A handsome German au pair who spoke perfect English. That was a surprise, but it didn't alter the fact that two small children had been left alone in a deserted park beside a stretch of water.

'I suppose you realise that Thomas could have been drowned?' she snapped.

He was leading the way through a beautiful conservatory full of hothouse blooms, and she thought how out of place she must appear in such surroundings with her limp wet hair and small pools of green water dripping from her clothes.

'Yes, I do,' he said contritely, 'but we had forgotten the bread for the ducks and the children were upset, so I dashed back for it, and. . .'

'I see. So you *were* with them originally,' she said, slightly mollified.

'But of course. I would never leave little Thomas and Jonathan for more than a second. I would be desolate if anything happened to them.'

Helen looked down on to herself. 'Yes, well, it nearly did. I'd like to speak to their parents. I think that Thomas will need antibiotics after being in the lake. There's bound to be bacteria in there, and it's unwise to risk him picking up an infection.'

He hesitated. 'Their father was late at the theatre and has given instructions he must not be disturbed.'

She frowned. 'And their mother?'

'She is no longer with us.'

'Well, in that case you will have to disturb the father,' she said flatly, 'and then I think I'll be on my way. I can clean up at my own place.'

They were in a lofty panelled hallway now and he stopped with his foot on the bottom rung of the stairs. He looked down at the child. 'Shall I perhaps get Thomas in the bath first?' he suggested.

'Yes, of course,' she agreed curtly, and the older boy ran upstairs after them. Helen looked around her. This was some house. It was a really beautiful place, but it was a house without a mother, and a father who mustn't be disturbed because he'd been socialising the night before. Well, he was going to have to know that his child required preventative medicine, and, although she imagined that the handsome au pair was capable of passing on the message, some perverse impulse made her decide she preferred to do it herself.

She was starting to shiver now, though, and didn't want to be hanging around much longer. A brisk run home would warm her up and after a hot bath she would be as good as new, but she would take antibiotics herself just as she had recommended them for the boy. No sense in taking any chances.

A door beside her was ajar and as she looked through it she saw a man asleep, sprawled across a large settee. The top button of his shirt was undone and his tie was askew. From where she was standing she could see that he was a big man, broad-shouldered, barrel-chested, yet trim with it. His hair was fair and silvering at the temples, and if his eyes had been open she could have bet on it that they'd be blue. There was stubble on his chin, and as his feet hung limply over the edge of the couch she saw that his shoes were where he'd kicked them off.

It was quite obvious that the man who could afford a German au pair, and had dispensed with his wife somewhere along the way, was sleeping off a hectic night. What a pity to have to waken him, she thought grimly.

As she squelched across the carpet Helen thought that in other company she might have been embarrassed at the sight she must look, but the man on the settee didn't look much better, and she *had* just pulled his little boy out of the lake.

When she reached his side and stood looking down upon him he opened his eyes suddenly like a man who was used to being brought quickly into wakefulness, and they *were* blue, incredibly so. What was more, they were full of surprise as he lay there observing her.

As Helen opened her mouth to speak he raised himself quickly on to one elbow and exclaimed, 'And who are *you*? You're soaking! What have you been up to?' His eyes were on her limp brown locks, her bare muddy feet, and the jogging-suit top clinging to her like a shroud.

Hazel eyes flashed as they looked into perplexed blue, and the words came tumbling out. 'Who I am is of no consequence, but what I've been up to is. I've just brought your little boy out of the lake in the park. He fell in when your — er — au pair went back to get some bread for the ducks. Apparently he'd only left them for a second, but anyone who has had any dealings with children knows that it only takes a second for them to get into trouble. I came back with them instead of rushing home to change because I wanted to impress upon you that Thomas will need antibiotics to counteract any ill effects from bacteria in the lake.'

Her eyes went over him as if she herself were immaculate, and she said crisply, 'Perhaps when you've had your *rest* you can see that he gets them. Your local GP will give you a prescription.'

There'd been alarm in the bright blue gaze when she'd mentioned the mishap in the park, but he was still staring at her in a bemused fashion, and when she'd said her piece he murmured slowly, 'And that's it, is it?'

Helen found herself colouring. There was just the faintest hint of irony behind the meek question. 'Er. . . yes, and now if you'll excuse me I'll be on my way.'

'Yes, indeed, and thank you for being there for my

son. Bruno needs eyes in the back of his head with those two young imps.'

He was on his feet now, looking even more crumpled. There were tired lines around his eyes, and Helen found that she barely came up to his shoulder.

'Yes, it would appear so,' she agreed coolly, and without more ado she swivelled on her heel and went.

As she hurried back through the park her indignation was submerged by curiosity. What a strange set-up that had been. All male, from the looks of it. The children's mother was no longer with them, the blond au pair had said. How could anyone bear to leave two such delightful little boys? she wondered. When she'd seen that frightened little face beside her in the water she had known that she would have given her own life to save his if need be. And yet their father was sleeping off the previous night's exertions, and she'd like to bet they didn't just include going to the theatre.

The park was still quiet and she was glad of it. Her clothes were ruined. So much for the designer jogging suit, she thought wryly. She'd never been in such a smelly mess in her life, and with every stride nearer to her own small abode the thought of hot water, soap and a good splash of antiseptic was something she couldn't wait to get to.

Inside her tiny kitchen Helen stripped off all her clothes and put them straight into the washing machine. Whatever the suit came out like, at least it would have lost its pungent odour, she thought, as she stood nymph-like watching the bath fill, and as she caught sight of her grimy face in the mirror she found herself smiling at the memory of the expression on the big man's face.

He had looked absolutely dumbfounded to find her standing dripping beside him, and all the time she'd been telling him what to do he had listened meekly. Yet he didn't look like someone who was used to being put right. In spite of the fact that he'd slept in his clothes, he'd had a sort of presence about him, as if the boot might be on the other foot, and he the one who was used to giving the orders.

Orange juice, cereal, and crisp golden toast followed her long soak, and food had never tasted better. She was ravenous after the morning's exertions, and she found herself wondering who did the cooking at the house by the lake. Would it be Bruno Hengist, or the man with the bright blue eyes?

When she'd finished eating Helen rang her father and caught him just as his surgery was finishing.

'Hello, love,' he said, his voice warming. 'This is an early call. Is everything all right? Not having second thoughts about the cottage, and thinking of coming back home?'

She laughed. 'No, you know I'm not. I've been under your feet long enough. Most daughters at my age would have been married long since, and have a house full of babies by now.'

'Yes, well, we know why that is, don't we?' he said gently, and she thought, Yes we do, but the pain isn't as bad as it was. Time *did* heal, and she hadn't rung him for a chat about the past. Her move into the cottage a couple of weeks ago was a way of showing her parents that her eyes were firmly fixed on the future, and, if they'd had any doubts about that, her absorption in her career in health care proved that she wasn't looking back any more, but surging forward with strength and determination.

'Can you let me have a prescription for penicillin, please?' she asked with a swift change of subject.

'Why? Aren't you well?' Malcolm Blake asked, back in his role of caring GP.

'No. I'm fine, Dad,' she assured him. 'It's just that while I was jogging through the park this morning I had occasion to jump in the lake and it was a bit smelly.'

'What?' She could visualise the bushy grey brows beneath his silver thatch arching in surprise and concern.

'A little boy fell in, and I was the only one around to fish him out.'

'And are you both all right?'

'Yes. I've told the parents, or perhaps I should say *parent*, to make sure he's given antibiotics to counteract any infection from bacteria in the water, and thought I'd better heed my own counsel.'

'Yes, of course,' he agreed briskly. 'Best not to take any chances. Jim will be doing the calls in your area this morning. I'll ask him to drop the prescription off, or better still pick up the tablets for you rather than have any delay.'

'Dad!' she protested mildly. 'I'll get them myself. Just ask him to pop it through the letter-box.'

He chuckled. 'He won't want to do that. He'll expect a coffee.'

She sighed. 'Yes, I know.'

'He's very fond of you. Your mother and I would like to see you settled.'

'Yes? Well, when Mr Right comes along you'll be the first to know,' she assured him with a rueful laugh.

'Point taken, daughter,' he conceded wryly, and it was his turn to sigh, but not for long. 'How about dinner tomorrow night to round off your vacation? It would please your mother.'

'Yes, of course,' she agreed readily. 'About eightish?'

'Sure, that'll be fine. I'll tell her to kill the fatted calf.'

'I've only been gone two weeks,' she protested laughingly.

'Is that all? It seems longer.'

Helen's heart twisted. She loved them dearly. Her father, the hardworking family doctor with his kind eyes and tired face, and her mother, small, dark-haired and tranquil. . .coping with the stresses of being headmistress of the beautiful spa town's biggest comprehensive.

That was one of the reasons why Helen had been in no rush to find a place of her own. '*You* put them back into one piece, and then they come to *me* to be taught,' her mother had sometimes said, as they discussed their respective involvement with children, both of them aware that, fulfilling though their work might be, it was hard. . .and continuous.

In the end it had been Margaret Blake's own suggestion for Helen to find a place of her own like the cottage by the side of Linnias Park. They'd noticed it one day when they'd been out for a stroll, and when her mother had seen the 'For Sale' notice outside the tiny stone cottage she'd said, 'That would be lovely for you, Helen. A place of your own, and yet not too far away from us.'

'I'm all right as I am, Mum,' she'd protested, but the older woman had said calmly,

'Do you like it?'

'Well, yes, of course I do. It's lovely.'

And it was. Built from golden Costwold stone, with bow windows at the front, it had an arched porch that led to a flower-filled garden, and at the back was a small lawn that sloped down to an orchard which was already showing signs of the harvest to come. The inside was just as appealing with a large, airy lounge, small

kitchen, two bedrooms and a tiny bathroom, all taste-
fully decorated in the tranquil shades that Helen loved
the most.

'Could you afford it,' was her mother's next question.

'Yes, I think so, but. . .'

'And you would be nearer to the hospital?'

'Quite a lot, yes.'

'And am I fully capable of coping without you?'

Helen's eyes had warmed. 'Yes, of course you are,
but your work at the school is so demanding I'm afraid
of you overdoing it. You did have that nasty attack of
shingles last year, don't forget.'

'Bless you for worrying about me, darling,' Margaret
Blake had said. 'Would it make you feel any better if I
told you that I've been thinking of retiring at the end of
the year?' and with a quick switch back to her brisk
inquisition, 'So there would be no problem. I want you
to have some breathing space. A place of your own
where you can do your own thing. . .unwind. . .have
your friends round without Dad and me always being
there. Right?'

The cottage really was lovely. She'd felt its pull, and
as excitement had started to rise inside her she'd said,
'If you're sure, Mum?'

Her mother had laughed. 'Haven't I just said so?'

And so she had bought it, and taken two weeks'
holiday to move in, and even though her father had
seemed just a little downcast she knew they were both
happy about the move, and if they were happy so was
she. In fact she was ecstatic.

James Deardon was her father's junior partner, a slim
red-haired young man, energetic, efficient, and just a
bit too managing for Helen's liking. There were times

when she thought he was under the impression that his position in the practice entitled him to prime time in the social life of his partner's daughter, and she felt that the time was fast approaching when she was going to have to put him right.

She would have preferred her father not to involve him in bringing the tablets to her, but he'd had it arranged before she'd had time to argue, and she could see that it would be a case of him bustling into her new home and familiarising himself with it almost before she'd had time to do so herself.

One good thing was that he wouldn't be asking when he could see her again, as he already knew. They would be in the same company that night. It was the annual fund-raising dinner-dance of the Friends of St Margaret's, and all the local medical fraternity would be there along with the charity organisers and staff from the hospital.

It was always a delightful evening, and Helen and her parents invariably attended to give their support and meet up with old friends, and this time she would be making her way there from her own home.

However, when he arrived, for once Jim Deardon had little to say. When she opened the door to him he put the tablets into her hand, and with a brief, 'I'm in one heck of a rush, Helen. Half the population must be ailing today. See you tonight, eh?' he was gone. . .to her great relief.

He'd taken her out a couple of times, and although he was hardly the most restful person in the world it had been pleasant enough, and she might have gone more often if he hadn't made such a point of monopolising her, and taking it for granted that she was about to succumb to his charms. But, of course, he wasn't to know that Adam Kerwin, who had been killed almost on the eve of their wedding in a climbing accident, was a very hard act to follow.

Helen was looking forward to the evening. It had been a hectic couple of weeks and she was ready to take up her social life again. Most of her hospital colleagues would be there and it would be nice to catch up on what had been happening in her absence. She only hoped that Jim wouldn't be hovering all the time, though 'hover' was perhaps hardly the word; his presence came over more like an onslaught.

When she was ready she inspected herself carefully in the mirror in her bedroom, and she found herself smiling at the recollection of how she'd looked earlier that morning. She could still see the dumbfounded expression of the man on the sofa as she'd stood beside him delivering her instructions to the accompaniment of a steady drip, drip on the carpet.

And just as easy on the memory was the bronzed, supple handsomeness of the youth called Bruno Hengist. The little ones had been memorable too — children always were — and there was a tight band of pain around her heart as she thought how her life was so full of them, and yet none was her own. The virginal white of the dress she had chosen for tonight wasn't just a hollow symbol in her case. It described her exactly, and she thought that wasn't how it would have been if Adam had lived.

Yes, but you've had plenty of opportunities since, haven't you? the voice of reason said, and she supposed she had, but, as she'd thought earlier, the man she'd loved was a hard act to follow.

When she appeared in the doorway of the banqueting suite at the town hall three pairs of eyes were immediately focused on her. Her father, chatting to a fellow GP, saw the slender dark-haired figure in the white dress and was filled with pride. His daughter had style and a graceful charm that was all her own, he thought fondly.

James Deardon's quick glance observed the arrival of the woman he had decided he was going to marry with a mixture of approval and irritation. She was everything he had always promised himself, but why did she always have to look so damned aloof?

At the opposite side of the room the man who had surveyed her in supine amazement in the lounge of the house by the park was filled with surprise again as he saw her framed between the marble pillars of the doorway.

'Well, well!' he murmured softly. 'If it isn't the lady of the lake!'

His companion, a tall, distinguished-looking elderly man with thinning grey hair, and dressed in an immaculate dinner-suit, heard him, and his eyes followed the other man's gaze.

'I'm not with you, old chap,' he said.

The big man grinned. 'The last time I saw the delectable-looking lady in white she was covered in pond-weed,' he said, 'and she was giving me a diatribe on the use of antibiotics. I certainly never expected to see her again so soon.'

'You didn't? If you're talking about Helen Blake, you're going to be seeing her all the time, I'm afraid. She's your registrar.'

CHAPTER TWO

UNAWARE that she was being observed, Helen moved across to where her mother was seated in conversation with Janice Makin, the nursing manager at St Margaret's.

'I've just been hearing about Hugh Copley's replacement,' Margaret Blake said with a warm smile of welcome as Helen dropped a kiss on her serene brow.

'Ah! So our long-awaited new paediatric surgeon has arrived at last?' she breathed. 'I don't know whether to be glad or sorry that I wasn't there to welcome him. What's he like, Jan?'

They were great friends, these two, often on opposite sides when staffing and other similar problems arose, but both totally appreciative of the other's skill and commitment.

The nursing manager was a wiry forty-year-old with close-cropped brown hair, laughing eyes of the same colour, and a rapier-like mind that was always working on behalf of her nurses. . .'my girls', as she was wont to describe them. Janice had teenage twin daughters and was often heard to say wryly that she didn't know who caused her the most brain-fag, 'her girls' or 'her girls'.

She knew that although it had been asked casually the question came from the depths of Helen's heart, and she paused a moment before answering. They were both aware that her friend would be in close daily contact with the man who had taken the place of the meticulous

Hugh Copley, and any conflict of personalities could be disastrous.

Helen had worked well with the man who had just hung up his stethoscope, even though she knew that Janice thought he was an old fusspot. The young registrar had a fanatical love of order and had coped with his pedantic ways without complaint. If she'd sometimes felt that the elderly surgeon wasn't as quick as he used to be, or not as *au fait* with new procedures as she would have liked, she'd kept it to herself, but she had been relieved when he'd decided to retire, and was fervently hoping that the younger man who was to replace him would have the same precision of manner and desire for orderliness as 'Sir Hugh', as he was known among the staff at St Margaret's, but with a new approach.

Janice was ready to answer her question and there was a mischievous twinkle in her eye as she said, 'From the moment Daniel Reed walked into the hospital he's had us all eating out of his hand. He's anything but handsome, yet the man's a real charmer. He's so easy and relaxed, nothing gets him down. The nurses have already christened him "Danny Boy", and the kids adore him. And, what is more, there doesn't appear to be a Mrs Reed.' She rolled her eyes wickedly. 'If I weren't so happy with my Ted I'd be getting ideas.'

Helen's smile was strained. Was Janice warning her about the new man? Breaking it to her gently that he was no fastidious Hugh Copley? Because if that was the case she wasn't sure that she could work with a laid-back popularity-seeker.

'But of course we're not all spoken for, are we?' said the unrepentant Janice. 'And I could think of someone who would be just what the doctor ordered. . .'

She had to laugh at that. 'Stop teasing, Janice. I

haven't even met the guy yet, and he sounds anything but my type.'

'Yes? Well, that omission is about to be rectified. Here he comes with old Copley.'

Helen found that she was holding her breath. She had the strangest sensation that the next few moments were going to be very important, but why? she asked herself. She hadn't got herself into a state when she'd first met Hugh Copley. There had been no need to. She knew her job and worked hard at it. . .no need to be nervous now, then. It was Janice's teasing that was affecting her.

She turned slowly and her eyes widened in disbelief. The man walking towards them with a relaxed, easy stride, nodding and smiling at other guests as he passed, was the father of Thomas and Jonathan. . .the man on the sofa. . .and he wasn't crumpled any more.

He wasn't crumpled, but neither was he dressed like anyone else. Among all the dark evening suits his lightweight beige jacket and trousers, cream shirt and brightly patterned tie stood out like a beacon. His skin was tanned, and his hair a thick honey-gold, brushed carelessly back from a face that was broad-browed and rugged, with a nose that wasn't quite straight and a wide, humorous mouth.

Arrival of the 'Sun King', she thought illogically as dismay filled her. Everything about him was golden. Beside him, 'Sir Hugh' looked like a stick-insect.

The stick-insect was speaking. 'Helen, let me introduce my sucessor. . . Daniel Reed.' And, turning to the big blond man, 'Helen Blake, your registrar, and a very competent one at that.'

As they shook hands his clasp was warm and firm and the arresting face momentarily serious, but there was a glint in the blue eyes that told her he hadn't forgotten the morning's episode — but then neither had she. The last thing she'd expected to come across on her morning run had been a child in danger, a male au pair, and a paediatric surgeon sleeping it off. But she hadn't known then who he was. Her face started to burn as she thought that if she had done she wouldn't have made such a thing about his taking precautions.

The staff at St Margaret's, and herself more than anyone, had been waiting a long time to meet this man. The appointment had been made as far back as eighteen months ago, but he'd had a commitment to a children's hospital in Australia, and had only recently become available.

There had been little information forthcoming regarding him except that he was a family man and a first-rate surgeon. The 'family man' part of it seemed to be correct up to a point, but one vital part of the family had seemed to be missing. There was no wife. . .no mother for those two bonny little boys. With regard to his medical skills — well, she would find out soon enough just how good he was.

'Grand to meet you, Helen,' he said with a brisk joviality, and in a murmur that only she heard, 'for the second time.' He raised his voice again. 'I seem to have been a long time getting here, but now that I'm finally back in England and at St Margaret's I don't think I shall have any regrets. It's good to be back among my fellow Brits.' And a shadow crossed his face for a fleeting second.

'It's nice to meet you too. I hope that you'll be happy with us at St Margaret's,' she said stiffly, aware that her mother and Janice were observing them with interest.

'Oh, have no fear, I will be,' he said breezily. 'I usually have no trouble slotting in wherever I am.' He gave a charming grin. 'Even though I *am* a bit on the big side.'

Yes, you are, she thought, you're larger than life. . . in every way. . .especially your ego. . .and then was immediately appalled at herself for judging him on such short acquaintance. But whatever she was right or wrong about there was one thing that was irrefutable: Daniel Reed and herself were as different as chalk from cheese, and they were going to be spending a lot of time in each other's company. . . It was a daunting thought.

Her glance went to Hugh Copley. They'd been a good team. What was *he* thinking about this self-contained newcomer? The older man had been such a stickler for detail and protocol, yet he seemed to be observing Daniel Reed with an amused benign approval, and she thought uneasily that he seemed to have charmed them all. . .with the exception of herself. . .but where were her manners?

She turned towards her mother, and as Margaret's smiling gaze met hers Helen said, 'I'm told you've already met Janice, but may I introduce my mother, Margaret Blake?'

He took Margaret's small hand in his and held it gently. 'Lovely to meet you, Mrs Blake.' And with a teasing smile, 'Am I to take it that the hospital was named after you?'

That caused laughter all round. Helen felt the weight of his charm once again, and wondered why, when everyone else was drooling over him, she should feel so disgruntled.

Perhaps he was aware of it and decided to break through her reserve, as he touched her arm briefly and said with a whimsical lift of the eyebrows, 'The band is playing good music. Shall we dance?' and before she could think of a reason not to she found herself on the small dance-floor in Daniel Reed's arms.

As his hold went around her Helen knew she didn't want close physical contact with this disturbing man. She was confused, off balance, and it was all because of this morning. . .or was it? Maybe it was because he was big and bouncy with lots of charm.

So far she'd had no desire for relationships with other men since Adam died. The loss had been so great she'd felt as if her heart had shrivelled into a dead dried-up shell, and the only things that made her come alive were St Margaret's and the small patients she treated there.

James Deardon was the only one who'd got anywhere near her, and that was because of two things; his tenacity, and Helen's awareness that as she wasn't terribly attracted to him the relationship wasn't going to hurt her in any way.

He was glaring at her now from across the floor where an elderly lady was bending his ear, and Helen knew he would be seething at the sight of her dancing with Daniel Reed.

As she matched her steps to those of her partner she thought that Jim had no need to worry. The new surgeon at St Margaret's wasn't her type. She was still reeling from the shock of discovering that the man with whom she was going to be working in close contact was the bleary-eyed slumberer of this morning.

Daniel Reed's eyes were on her, watching her, sizing her up, and he said softly, 'You're very preoccupied. . . Miss Blake.'

Helen eyed him back. 'Am I? I was wondering how Thomas is.' It was true, she was, but she'd thrown the question at him to take his attention off herself.

'He's fine. No apparent after-effects. I really am most

grateful for what you did. I'm usually with the boys myself at that hour, but I'd been up most of the night and I just flaked when I got in.'

'Yes — er — Bruno. . .your au pair. . .said that you'd been to the theatre.' There was disapproval in her voice. Helen knew it and she couldn't help it.

'Mmm. I was called out at ten o'clock. . .an appendicectomy, small girl of two years old.'

Helen felt her jaw drop. 'You were *in* Theatre?' she questioned weakly. 'At St Margaret's? You weren't out on the town?'

Fair brows were escalating in comic disbelief. 'So that's what you thought!' He gave an amazed chuckle. 'Fat chance? This is the first time I've socialised in ages, and I'm not sorry I came.'

Her colour rose. What did he mean by that? 'Obviously it was an emergency if the house officer called *you* out,' she said, bringing the conversation back on to an impersonal footing.

'Yes. The GP had seen her twice during the day and wasn't happy about her. He did the right thing by getting her to St Margaret's without delay. Distended abdomen, slightly febrile, coated tongue — you know the symptoms. No sign of respiratory infection or pain when I examined the abdomen, but a rectal examination had her in great discomfort. It was obvious that the appendix had descended behind the caecum.'

'Perforated?'

'Yes.' His face was sober. 'It's still a damned serious thing if neglected. In spite of all the excellent techniques we have today, appendicitis can be a killer.'

'I agree,' she said sombrely, at ease with him now they were united in a common bond. 'When I first came to St Margaret's we had a toddler admitted with it after days of neglect by the parents and dithering by the GP. By the time he got to us it was too late. It had been diagnosed as gastro-enteritis, but of course it wasn't, and peritonitis was well established.'

He nodded. 'Yes, well this little one came through it all right, and now she's on gentamicin and metronidazole. You approve?'

Helen stared at him. He was asking her opinion! During all the years she'd worked with Hugh Copley he'd never deferred to her once, and here was this new guy asking if she approved. Well, of course she did, but was he testing her. . .or joking perhaps?

'Yes, of course,' she said stiffly, and for a second there was puzzlement in his eyes, but it was gone in an instant and he said solemnly,

'By the way, we got the antibiotics for Thomas per your instructions.'

Her face flamed. 'I wasn't to know who you were, was I?' But I do now she thought. . . I surely do now.

He gave his easy grin. 'Exactly, but you cared enough to make the point,' and before she could reply to that he was asking, 'Who's the red-headed fellow glaring at us?' as they passed Jim Deardon. 'Friend of yours?'

'Yes.' She'd no intention of going into details.

'Really? I wouldn't like to see the way your enemies behave, then!' His smile took any sting out of the words but it didn't stop her from feeling foolish.

'He's — er — not — er. . .' She was stammering like some inarticulate teenager. 'He's probably wanting to chat,' she finished lamely.

'Yes?'

The music stopped at that moment and he escorted her back to where her parents and Janice were still conversing with Hugh Copley. The elderly surgeon took him by the arm. 'If you'll excuse us, I want to introduce Daniel to some more of the folks he needs to meet.'

'Sure,' he said easily, 'whatever you say, Hugh,' and to Helen standing tensely beside him, 'I believe you're back on Monday. I'll see you then. By the way, where do you live? Obviously somewhere near the park.'

'Yes, I have a cottage at the opposite side to yourself.'

'Really? Do you want a lift home?'

'She'll be going home with me,' a cool voice said at her elbow, and James placed a possessive arm around her waist.

Anger rose inside her. How dared he presume that he had a claim on her? But she could hardly start haranguing him in front of Daniel Reed, could she?

'Fine. I'll see you on the wards, then, Helen,' he said easily, and sauntered off with Hugh Copley at his side.

When he had gone, her pent-up feelings broke free and she rounded angrily on James. 'I make my own decisions,' she said coldly, 'and as I came alone I intend to go home alone. I don't require an escort so don't push it, please.'

'OK, OK,' he said stonily. 'It's just that I thought we'd be spending the evening together, and the moment you arrive that pushy new fellow from St Margaret's takes over.'

'No one has taken me over, as you so charmingly put it,' she said in a milder tone, 'so let's forget it, eh? They've just announced that the meal is about to be served. Shall we go in?'

He smiled, mollified that they were going to eat together, and for the rest of the evening she stayed with him, not so much as to placate him as to keep herself out of the radius of Mr Nice Guy.

* * *

On Monday morning Helen slept late, something she hadn't done for years. When she opened her eyes beneath the eaves of her charming bedroom she realised that she hadn't heard the alarm.

She was out of bed in a flash, groaning as she thought that she'd been in the park as early as seven o'clock during her holiday, when time was not of the essence, and now, today, when it was paramount, she'd overslept.

With five minutes to spare she slid the Golf GTI that had been last year's extravagance into her parking spot, and felt proud of her efforts. She was hot and sticky from rushing, but her usual immaculate self, the dark cap of her hair neat and shining, light make-up on a face that had a grave, tranquil charm of its own. The events of Saturday had diminished the tranquillity somewhat, but she was determined not to let the breezy newcomer get her flustered again.

Helen had a reputation at St Margaret's for being precise, efficient and absorbed in the job. If some of the staff felt it wasn't easy to get through her reserve — that she was a bit stand-offish — they let it pass. She'd had a bad time like lots of other folks, and everybody reacted to tragedy in different ways. Pity to shut herself away from happiness, but then it came in lots of different guises, and who was to say that she *hadn't* found hers?

She knew what was said, and supposed that she might be a bit intimidating at times, but she'd loved Adam dearly. They'd been friends at school, teenage sweethearts, and it had progressed from there. When he'd been killed she'd had to get on without him as best she could, and it had been very hard. Time had lessened the pain, but the emptiness was always there, and so far she hadn't met anyone who she felt could fill the aching void inside her.

The crisp pink cotton blouse and grey flannel skirt she'd dressed in would be cool and comfortable beneath her white coat, and the flat black shoes would take the strain off the part of the body that suffered the most with anyone connected with health care.

As Helen bent over the back seat of her car to collect her belongings an old black Rover that had seen better days chugged into the parking space next to her, and through the window she saw Daniel Reed behind the wheel.

The face that hadn't been out of her mind since their damp encounter in the house by the lake broke into a smile, and he raised his hand in cheerful salute before easing himself out of the car.

'You on the deadline too?' he said as he in turn collected his things, and then, stepping back in exaggerated surprise, 'That's a very trendy car for a. . .'

'An untrendy person?' she suggested coolly.

He threw back his head and laughed, and *she* sighed. He was even good-tempered and cheerful at this time of day, and the fact was making her all the more prickly.

'No. I was about to say it was a very trendy car for a respectable registrar, and if that isn't pure poetry I don't know what is.'

She wanted to laugh, even though it did make her sound like someone who wore woollen knee-socks and carried a big bottle of pills! He really was a very humorous man, but he made her uneasy. Perhaps it was because of the way they'd met — she didn't know — or perhaps it was because she'd let herself get too staid and serious. . .all work and no play making Helen a dull girl?

He started striding towards the big swing doors of the hospital and, having little alternative, she fell in beside him. The last thing she'd planned on her first day back was arriving in the company of her new senior colleague. She would have enough of his company as the day progressed, but if she hung about in the car park she would be late, and she didn't want that either.

As they walked along the main corridor together Helen felt the familiar pull of St Margaret's. This was her place. . .where she was happiest, among the small sufferers who came into her care, and she was hoping that the man beside her felt the same. On the face of it he was casual. . .easygoing. . .a charmer. . .which was all very nice, but it was the job that counted, and up to now she wasn't sure that Daniel Reed was right for St Margaret's. . .or as a senior colleague.

At the door of the consulting suite he paused. 'Come and see what I've been up to,' he invited, and as he pushed the door open her eyes widened.

The embossed wallpaper and thick carpeting that Hugh Copley had insisted on was gone, and pale cream walls were graced with attractive children's prints. The floor had been polished and brightly coloured rugs scattered upon it. Two tropical-fish tanks glowed in brilliant movement, and on a bench beneath the window were toys and computer-type games.

It was exactly the kind of room to put a nervous child or apprehensive parent at their ease, and her heart lifted. Daniel Reed might be a breed of consultant she hadn't come across before, but he certainly wasn't lacking in vision.

He was waiting for her reaction, eyes bright with curiosity, and on a perverse impulse she said drily,

'Whose arm have you been twisting to get all this? Our manager watches his budget like a hawk.'

It was an ungracious thing to say, and when she saw the disappointment in his face Helen wanted to take back the words, but it was too late.

'No arm-twisting involved, I assure you,' he said with a crisp impersonality that was unlike his previous manner. 'I brought the stuff in myself.'

'It's very nice,' she said lamely, knowing that after what she'd already said it sounded inane and empty.

'Yes, well, having kids of my own, I know what they like,' he said briefly, 'and, talking of children, I suggest we do the ward rounds together this morning so that I can fill you in with what's been happening while you've been away, and *you* can put me in the picture with anything I need to know.'

'Fine,' she agreed, 'and theatre rota as before?' That had been Monday, Wednesday, and Friday afternoons, apart from emergencies.

'No. I prefer mornings. . .for both of us.'

'But Mr Copley. . .'

'Do I look like Copley, Helen?' he asked with a bland sort of calm that could have been disguising indifference. . .or maybe annoyance.

'Er. . .no. . .of course not.'

'All right, then. The king is dead! Long live the king! I'll see you on the wards at ten-thirty.' And she was dismissed.

And that has put you in your place, Dr Blake, she thought grimly as she made her way to the staffroom. The king is dead, indeed! Danny Boy's silver tongue had a spiky edge to it. Yet he'd transformed the consulting suite in just two weeks, and how often had *she* thought that surgery should be early in the day so that tiny stomachs weren't left empty too long?

Helen shook her head in disbelief. In the space of five minutes she had been less than enthusiastic about two of Daniel Reed's innovations, and he in turn had let her see that, Mr Nice Guy or not, he was no push-over.

There were two junior house officers and a senior in the staffroom. The juniors—Mike Norton, a lanky, curly-haired lad from Lancashire, whose two obsessions in life were his motorbike and the pursuit of sleep, and John Travers, a plump forty-five-year-old, who had opted to come into health care later in life—greeted her with friendly enthusiasm.

'Enjoyed being out on parole, Helen?' Mike asked with a cheeky grin.

'Yes, it was lovely, thanks,' she said with a smile.

'House up to expectations?'

'Yes, super.'

'Have you met the new member of the hierarchy yet?' John asked.

'Yes again.' And that was the understatement of the year.

'Great, isn't he?' Mike enthused. 'He'll do for me any time!' He hadn't exactly been one of Hugh Copley's favourites and she could imagine Daniel Reed's *bonhomie* appealing to him.

The third member of the trio hadn't spoken. She'd given Helen a brief nod when she'd entered and continued to apply bright red lip gloss on to a full, pouting mouth, but at the mention of the new paediatric surgeon she joined in.

'He's really dishy!' she said, and as Helen looked at Jill Morrison's pert face with its smooth translucent skin and long-lashed grey eyes she thought that the curly-haired blonde wouldn't have missed anything about the newcomer. She would have seen his assets lined up like soldiers on parade; he was charismatic, wealthy, and a senior member of staff, all things that would appeal to a clever senior house officer who seemed to have completed her training at twice the speed of light compared to her own years of painstaking study. And as for Daniel Reed she'd like to bet that he wouldn't have shown any surprise at seeing *Jill* arrive in a red Golf.

'Yeah, been getting on like a house on fire, our Jilly and Danny Boy,' Mike chuckled. 'I can't see anybody else getting a look-in.'

As Jill reached up to take her white coat off the peg she gave him a playful push. 'You're only jealous because I prefer the desirable widower to you.'

Widower? The word hung in the air. She could hear the handsome au pair saying that the children's mother was no longer with them, and for some reason it had never occurred to her that it might be for the most irrevocable reason of all.

Helen sank down on to the nearest chair. As far as Jill was concerned that must surely be the biggest asset of all, and as regards herself. . .so far she hadn't got one single thing right about him. Was it going to go on like that?

By half-past ten Helen had brought herself up to date on the paperwork that had accumulated during her absence, had a chat with Alison Graham, a physiotherapist who was working on one of the patients, managed a quick cup of coffee, and was at the entrance to Pinocchio Ward on the dot.

But Daniel Reed was there before her, just inside the door chatting to the sister in charge, by the looks of it his good humour restored, and when he caught sight of her he said briskly, 'Hi, Helen. Let's get cracking, shall we? I want to see how the little dolly mixtures have been faring over the weekend.'

'Yes, by all means,' she agreed coolly, and with the thought inside her that she'd been walking these wards a long time in the role of consort. Now a new king was on the throne, and he could turn out to be the best. . .or the worst. . .thing that had ever happened to St Margaret's.

He appeared to be a breezy extrovert with lots of charm, and she'd like to wager he wouldn't be averse to bending the rules when it suited him. Meticulous and dedicated herself, could she cope with someone like that. . .a dolly mixture doctor?

CHAPTER THREE

DANIEL REED was already at the first bed holding a small hand in his. 'And how's this young fellow, Sister?' he asked as a small boy eyed him warily.

'Not very happy, I'm afraid,' she said. 'Feels he's here on sufferance.'

He chuckled. 'Can't blame him for that, can we?'

Helen saw from the boy's case-notes that he had been admitted the previous day for a tonsillectomy. She'd already seen his name on her list for the theatre tomorrow, and when Daniel Reed had finished chatting to him she intended examining his throat.

'*My* name's Daniel Reed. What's yours?' the big fair-haired man was asking him.

'Philip,' was the sulky response.

'Well, Philip, Dr Blake here is going to make your throat better tomorrow. . .just a small operation and you won't have any more of those nasty sore throats.'

He was rewarded with a scowl. 'My friend Jason says it'll hurt. I don't want an operation. I want to go home!'

'You will, son, very soon,' he said reassuringly, and to Helen, 'He's down on the list for tomorrow morning. . . Philip Curtis.'

'Yes, I know,' she murmured, giving the reluctant patient a friendly smile. 'I'm up to date on paperwork and schedules.'

'I thought you might be.'

It could have been a compliment, but she didn't think it was. 'Would you rather I weren't?' she asked stiffly.

He swivelled to face her. 'No, of course not,' he said evenly. 'It's just that Hugh Copley was singing your praises most of Saturday evening, so much so that I was almost afraid of teaming up with such a paragon.'

A complimentary remark. . .so why did it sound like a reprimand?

He was moving towards the next bed, and when she'd dealt with Philip Helen followed him. Joanne Carter wasn't a new admission. She was anorexic, and extremely cunning and uncooperative with it. The thirteen-year-old daughter of well-to-do parents, she had reacted to stress in the home, and when her weight had reached a dangerous level she had been brought into St Margaret's to save her life.

Helen felt heart-sorry for the petulant mixed-up child and always stopped to chat with her even though, strictly speaking, she was not in her care. Joanne had been moved into a surgical ward because the paediatrician felt her to be a disrupting influence among the small long-stay patients.

Monitoring her food intake and the prevention of induced vomiting were having results and she had regained a little of her weight loss, but Helen was aware that the child's mental attitude to the problem was the biggest barrier to her recovery. She was desperately in need of counselling and a child psychiatrist was visiting her regularly.

Her hollow little face crumpled when she saw the dark-haired doctor, and she shrilled, 'Where've you been? I've missed you!'

The young registrar's arm went around the child's thin shoulders and Helen held Joanne to her, stroking the mop of dark curls. 'I've been on holiday, Joanne.

Remember? I told you I was going to be off for two weeks. Had you forgotten?'

'I don't know. I suppose I must have,' she wailed. 'I keep telling you that every day is like a week here, away from school and all my friends.'

Helen noticed there was no pining for the parents. . . especially the father.

'Your friends come to see you, don't they?' she said gently.

'Yes, but it's not the same, is it?'

'No, it's not, but you're the only one who can put that right. If you eat up everything you're given we'll have you home in no time, and now, if you promise to tuck into your dinner when it comes, I've got something for you.'

Green eyes showed just the faintest sparkle. 'You have?'

'Yes. The Jason Donovan tape you wanted, and a little surprise present as well.'

She took a small neatly wrapped parcel out of the pocket of her white coat and placed it into the girl's hands. 'You can tell me tomorrow if you like it.'

Daniel Reed had stood without speaking during the discourse between them, his keen glance taking in the young girl's appearance and the expensive toiletries on her locker. His eyes flicked over the silk pyjamas that were too old and sophisticated for her emaciated body, and he frowned.

'That little dolly mixture seems to have her problems,' he murmured as they moved on.

Helen's face tightened. 'Yes. There seems to be no lack of money, clothes, teenage toys in the home, but love seems to be in short supply. Mother a bit flighty and father handy with his fists.' She sighed. 'I've got such wonderful parents, my heart bleeds for those who haven't.'

'And what about kids who have only one parent?' He'd said it mildly, but she had a feeling he needed to know the answer.

The huge hazel eyes that dominated her face surveyed him gravely. '*I'm* hardly in a position to pass an opinion, am I? But I'd say it would depend on the quality of the one remaining parent.'

'And what sort of a grading would a guy get who let his son fall into the lake?' he asked with a wry lift of the eyebrow.

'Initially not very high,' she said quietly, 'but the circumstances are not always known to the person doing the grading, are they?'

'True. So can I take it that I've been upgraded?'

There was a mischievous gleam in his eye and she thought, He makes me sound like a fussy schoolmarm, but the ward sister was waiting for them at the next bed, watching them curiously, and no doubt wondering what they were discussing, and so her reply had to be brief. 'Just a little,' she murmured.

The child was asleep, fine silver hair splayed across the pillow like a silken cobweb, small fists clenched and uneasy.

'Suzanne, the appendicectomy,' he said briefly, and to the hovering nurse, 'How's she been, Sister?'

'Fretful, Mr Reed. Doesn't like the tube.'

'Hmm. Any infection from the incision?'

'No, not so far.'

'Good.'

'The mother has been with her ever since the operation, but now that the child is sleeping properly for the first time she's gone to get some rest herself.'

Daniel lifted the sheets back and examined the sleeping child gently. She whimpered in her sleep but didn't wake, and when he'd finished he gave a satisfied nod.

'The nasogastric tube can come out tomorrow,' he said.

'Very good, Mr Reed,' Sister murmured.

As they stopped at the various beds Helen was ashamed of her earlier critical attitude. He was efficient, caring, kind, in an easy, relaxed sort of way. There was a lessening of the tension inside her, and as they crossed the corridor into Pluto Ward her heart was lifting. It was going to be all right. She could feel it in her bones.

Jalal Ashram was in Pluto Ward. It was his progress that she'd discussed earlier with the physiotherapist, and when he saw them his dark young face broke into a smile.

'I've been swimming and it doesn't hurt, Dr Blake!' he cried excitedly. Helen gave him one of her rare brilliant smiles in return.

'That's great, Jalal. I've been talking to Alison and she's very pleased with you. And what about the pain the rest of the time?'

'Not as bad as it was.' His eyes went to Daniel standing beside her. 'The new doctor brought me fruit and chapatis while you were away.'

'Well! I see!' As she swung round in surprise Daniel hid his face behind his hand like a small boy caught in the act, and in the eye that remained uncovered there was amusement.

Helen found herself smiling. She couldn't imagine 'Sir Hugh' coming in with chapatis. The only thing she'd ever seen *him* dole out had been a boiled sweet, wrapped, of course, and she'd felt he expected the recipient to touch the forelock. But how was Daniel finding time for all these little gestures? He had his commitment to St Margaret's. . .and two small boys to cope with.

'Bruno is an excellent shopper,' he said, with what was beginning to look like an uncanny ability to read her mind, and then switching to the more important topic of the child's health, 'I see this young man has been with us for some time.'

'Yes. He had experienced some weight loss, had intermittent fever and pain in the joints, though the pain was more recent than the other symptoms. Tests indicated Stills Disease. . .pauciarticular. It's the first time we've treated a boy. Previous cases have all been girls. We had discussed joint replacement, but because of his extreme youth had hesitated, and in the meantime he's having the usual treatment for chronic juvenile arthritis.'

'Aspirin, night splints, and physiotherapy?'

'Yes.'

'Good. Obviously we'll need to keep an eye on him. Knees are in a poor state, but as you say he's got a lot of growing to do, and joint replacement would have to be given careful thought.'

By the time they had vetted the new admissions, those at intermediate stages of recovery, and the lucky ones about to be discharged, it was lunchtime, and they separated, Helen to the staff dining-room, and Daniel Reed to the privacy of his office, where she surmised he would have his meal sent in as Hugh Copley had always done.

Helen carried her tray of food to an empty table and sat down thankfully. A solitary meal was just what she needed. Time to eat, and at the same time gather her

thoughts about the first morning spent with the ebullient
Daniel Reed. His was a difficult personality to pin
down. On the face of it he was carefree, casual in his
approach, flippant almost, and yet out there on the
wards this morning she couldn't have doubted his
commitment.

The moment of peace was short-lived. As she picked
up her knife and fork Helen heard the deep rumble of a
man's laugh and the lighter tones of a woman's. When
she turned it was to see Daniel Reed and Jill Morrison
seating themselves at a table behind her. The senior
house officer looked glowing and seductive and Helen
wondered where *she'd* spent the morning. Certainly not
using any brain or muscle from the looks of her, she
thought irritably.

Jill was bright, one of the smartest house officers
they'd had in a long time, and she was also crafty, which
meant being on the back row when the work was being
doled out. Mike and John were two good lads, but Jill
always had an eye to the main chance.

Yet the affable Daniel seemed to like her company,
and in fairness to him he'd hardly had time to judge.
Perhaps that was how he was. . .matey with everybody.
And how did he see her, she wondered. . .nobody's
friend? Had she mourned Adam so much and for so
long that she was afraid to let anyone else into her life?

Forget him, she told herself firmly as she ploughed
through a mediocre salad. The man is nothing to
you. . .or you to him.

In the afternoon he called a meeting of junior and senior
officers, and herself. There was just a brief phone call to
say, 'Can you come along to my office, Helen? Now that
you're back I thought we'd have a quick natter to see

how you all tick, and for anyone who has anything to say to get it off their chest.'

And what was that supposed to mean? That he was aware that she was critical of him?

'Yes, of course, I'll be right along,' she said crisply.

There was a moment's silence, as if he might have been expecting a show of enthusiasm, but when it wasn't forthcoming he just said, 'Fine,' and put down the receiver.

'Informal', she thought. Well, it would have to be, wouldn't it? She didn't think Daniel Reed would know how to stand on ceremony, and if he told them that he wanted them to be one big happy family as they slogged on the wards and in the theatre she would explode. All of them, even Jill, knew what they were about, and they coped with long hours and stress as if to the manner born, and, that being so, they could do without any banal platitudes.

When she strode into his office looking calm and unruffled, having flicked a brush through the dark cap of her hair, and applied fresh pale pink lip gloss, the others were already assembled, and immediately her calm disintegrated as she realised that she'd been the last to be summoned.

'Hi, Helen,' he said cheerfully, and pointing to the vacant seat beside him, 'Take a pew.' But she had already decided that she'd rather be facing him than sideways on, and so she ignored the invitation and dropped on to a chair at the back.

If he was aware of the snub Daniel Reed didn't show it. He went straight to the point of the meeting. 'I've delayed this get-together until Helen Blake was back among us,' he said with easy authority, 'and now that she's here we'll proceed. There is still one member of our small nucleus missing. Joan Emmerson, the paediatrician, is unwell with a virus, but, apart from that, all of us who are doctors on Pinocchio and Pluto Wards are here.'

There was a pause as his clear blue glance went over each of them in turn, and when it rested on her Helen gave him a tight smile. It wasn't easy to ignore his magnetic charm. As she'd already admitted to herself, it was quite unnerving. Maybe that was why she was finding fault with him all the time. . .because she wanted him to be a clone. . .a stereotype doctor. . .she could cope with that rather than an unknown quantity, but if that really *was* the situation then it was high time she got herself sorted out.

He leant back in the big swivel chair behind his desk and said, 'As you're all aware, I've only been back in this country a short time, and at St Margaret's for just a couple of weeks, and I want to take this opportunity of saying how much I appreciate the way you've made me so welcome.'

Helen felt her face burn. *She* hadn't exactly put out the red carpet, had she? And unless he was unbelievably thick-skinned he must be aware of it.

'You'll be seeing plenty of me,' he was saying. 'I will be here four days out of the five. Fridays I will be at my consulting-rooms in the centre of the town, but for the rest of the week I will be here at St Margaret's, and I hope that we're going to make a good team. I want to impress upon you at this point that there will be nothing too small that I would not want to hear about if it is for the good of our patients or the hospital. Do please bear that in mind. If any of you here have anything that you would like to ask me, or consult me about, or have any comment you wish to make. . .please feel free to do so.

'Steve Barrett, your excellent manager, tells me that St Margaret's has applied to become a trust hospital as from April next year in the third wave. Instead of being directly managed, it will be splitting from the Health Authority to do its own budgeting and contracting with medical authorities outside the area.

'I don't doubt that there are mixed feelings among you regarding this. My own personal opinion from what I've heard in the short time I've been back is that the financial side of health care should be left to the managers, and *we* should be allowed to get on with the job for which we've been trained. . .providing and developing medical services in the hospital where we are employed.'

There was a murmur of agreement but Helen didn't join in. She was of the firm belief that if St Margaret's were given the chance to control its own finances it would be in a position to provide vastly improved resources for its medical staff.

She was conscious of Daniel Reed watching her, reading her thoughts, no doubt, and as if in confirmation he said with a smile, 'Perhaps our registrar will give us *her* opinion?'

'I'm afraid I must disagree with Mr Reed,' Helen said quietly. 'I'm all for St Margaret's becoming a trust. I think that the benefits will be really worthwhile when you consider the reputation of the hospital, and how we will be able to develop the facilities here even more when we control our own finances. Our management will be able to use money paid to us for contracts from other authorities in whatever way they choose. If there is any surplus they will be able to hold it over from year to year if they so desire to provide services in different areas, or utilise it to instigate new services where needed, all of which will be much easier within a trust.

'It's the long-term view that counts in something like this, not what we might think is right for just this moment.'

He gave a rueful shrug when she'd finished. 'So there you are — two opinions. Helen and I seem to be on different wavelengths.' There was something in his tone that told her he wasn't just referring to the trust situation either.

'How about the rest of you? What do you think?' he asked, and that set the ball rolling. For the next half-hour there was non-stop, sometimes heated discussion on the subject, and if Daniel hadn't called a halt it would have gone on indefinitely.

When the meeting was over and Helen rose to leave she found Daniel beside her. 'We agree to differ, then?' he said with a lop-sided smile that made her wish he wouldn't be so darned pleasant about everything.

'It would appear so,' she said abruptly.

And as Jill Morrison came up behind him he said with a gravity foreign to him, 'Maybe we'll get it right. . . eventually.'

As she walked back along the corridor to the staff-room Helen realised, with an odd little pain around her heart, that for them to get it right was what she wanted, and so far her every gesture, every word, was pushing the possibility further away.

CHAPTER FOUR

WHEN she got back to the cottage in the early evening Helen changed into a cotton sundress before preparing her evening meal. The heat of the day was past but the July sun was still high in the sky, and once she'd eaten she intended spending a couple of hours in the garden. There was quite a lot of tidying up to be done, but tonight she was just going to lie in the hammock beneath the trees.

She was restless and on edge, and knew why. Her peaceful existence had been invaded by a charismatic Viking, a big fair man who was bringing her senses to life. The senses that had been numbed ever since Adam had been taken from her, and it was a strange feeling, especially so as ninety-nine per cent of the time she disapproved of him. It was that other one per cent that was the cause of her unease, and as she eased herself carefully into the hammock she vowed that she was going to unwind, let the peace of the quiet garden help to untangle her nerve-ends.

'You're making something out of nothing,' she told herself aloud as the book she'd taken out with her lay unread on her lap. 'Daniel Reed is probably being extra chummy because of the lake episode. That's how people behave when they're indebted to someone and wish they weren't. Just relax, woman. For heaven's sake, relax!'

And, surprisingly, she did. As the warmth and solitude wrapped themselves around her, and the hammock swung gently to and fro, she started to doze with the big straw hat that she wore in the garden tilted over her face.

A cacophony of bicycle bells broke into her consciousness and she lay there drowsily wondering where the sound was coming from, but she was instantly awake when a voice said from beside her, 'I hate to do it, because you look so peaceful lying there, but I'm afraid it's my turn to disturb *your* slumbers this time.'

Helen slowly lifted the hat from off her face, and for one long amazed moment her beautiful hazel eyes looked up at Daniel, and then she pulled herself quickly upright, in her confusion forgetting that a hammock was a thing to be treated with respect if one didn't want to end up in a heap on the floor.

It tilted precariously, and in the second that it spewed her out Daniel Reed caught her in his arms. It would have been hard to say who was the most surprised, and as he looked down on her Helen thought, If he makes a joke of it or laughs I shall want to curl up and die. But he didn't.

She saw a sudden hunger in his eyes. Not the hunger of a starving man, more the look of one who was used to a meagre diet and suddenly saw a banquet before him. He took a deep breath, and she was aware of his arm against the bare skin of her back. It felt warm and secure, and as he gently set her on her feet it stayed around her.

'That was my fault. I startled you,' he said contritely. 'I really am most sorry.'

Helen smiled, and it wasn't the tight-lipped variety that she'd been subjecting him to, but her natural unaffected beam. 'It's all right. No harm done. You just caught me napping, that's all.'

'I wonder,' he murmured as his arm fell away.

'What?'

'Whether any harm *has* been done.' And then, as if bringing his mind back to basics, he pointed to the high laurel hedge that separated her garden from the park. 'Bruno and the boys are out there. We all came over on our bikes to bring you something,' and, raising his voice, he called, 'Thomas!'

When the little boy came running down the path he was carrying a parcel, and his older brother and the stunning German were close behind.

'Tell Helen why we're here, Thomas,' Daniel Reed commanded.

'We've brought you this,' he said shyly as he thrust the package at her.

'For me?' she exclaimed with a surprised glance at the man beside him.

'Yes, for you,' the child repeated, and when she stood there making no attempt to unwrap it, 'Aren't you going to open it?'

'Well, of course,' she said quickly, controlling her amazement, and she removed the wrapping paper with all possible speed.

Her eyes widened when she saw the contents. It was a jogging suit, the same brand, same colour as the one she'd been wearing when she'd plunged into the lake, and she was touched at the gesture.

Helen bent down swiftly and kissed Thomas's smooth brown cheek. 'What a lovely thought,' she said gravely. 'I'll think of you every time I wear it, Thomas.'

He gave a pleased grin and Jonathan nudged him from behind. 'Tell her it was Dad's idea.'

She heard him and the glow of pleasure within her increased. 'Whoever the idea came from it was a very nice thought,' she said tactfully, 'and as you've all made a special journey to bring it I think the least I can do is offer you some refreshment.' She looked down on to the two small fair heads. 'Perhaps a Coke or lemonade?'

'Yes, please,' they chorused. 'It's hot in the park!'

Helen's glance went to the two men standing beside them, both just as fair and tanned as the children. One a smiling youth, and the other broad-shouldered, relaxed, and very memorable, a man in every sense of the word, and her heart lifted.

With the exception of her parents, and James who had made only a doorstep call, this all-male quartet were her first visitors, the first ones to cross her threshold, and just a few short days ago the last thing she would have expected was to be entertaining two very presentable men and two small boys.

'You're my first visitors,' she said with a smile, and with generous humour, 'and you've presented me with quantity as well as quality. Do come inside,' and she led the way into her sitting-room.

Daniel Reed looked around him as they all trooped inside. 'Mmm, very nice,' he said approvingly. 'Obviously you're a lady of taste. Are we to take it that you live here alone, Helen?'

'Yes, there's just me,' she said airily as she motioned for them to sit down. 'No live-in lovers. . .or staff. . . just a stray pussycat called Forceps for company.'

His deep laugh rang out. 'Forceps?'

'Yes, because he's always trying to hook things out of the fridge.'

As she went into the kitchen with the boys close behind Bruno uncoiled himself off the sofa and followed them.

'You look very different from that other time, Helen,' he said in his precise, stilted English.

Her smile flashed out. 'You mean without the pond-weed in my hair?'

He smiled back, showing dazzling white teeth. 'Yes, indeed.'

'Hmm, well, that would have to be an improvement, wouldn't it?' And with the children eyeing her expectantly she opened the fridge.

When they had both been served with a tall glass of lemonade and a cookie she turned to Bruno. 'And what can I get you?'

'The lemonade will do very well, thank you,' he said, and when she'd poured him a glass and pointed to the cookie jar Helen went in search of Daniel Reed.

She found him standing by the window with a photograph of Adam in a polished wooden frame in his hands, and as he turned to face her the rays of the setting sun behind him turned the silver and gold of his hair into pale flame, and threw the rugged contours of his face into shadow.

'I recognise the face,' he said slowly as his gaze left hers and went back to the photograph. 'It's Adam Kerwin, the mountaineer, isn't it?'

Helen nodded bleakly.

He was watching her face. 'Were you acquainted?'

'Yes,' Helen told him steadily as he replaced the photograph carefully in its place. 'I think I could say that. We were engaged. . .due to be married a month after that last climb. . .but of course it didn't happen. Adam never came back. He's still lying at the bottom of an unapproachable chasm in the Himalayas.'

Compassion, and something that could have been anger, kindled in the bright blue eyes, and Daniel said softly, 'You poor lass. I remember it happening. At that time his name was a household word.' And then the anger that she'd sensed came through. 'But why the hell did he have to attempt a climb like that when he was about to get married? He would know the risks.'

Helen stared at him. He was the only person who had ever passed censure on Adam. Everyone, even her parents to a lesser degree, had seen the tragedy as a sad example of the hazards of mountaineering, and the timing of it had seemed of less importance than the loss of one of the country's most able climbers.

But there had been times in the darkest hours of the night when Helen had asked herself in recurring anguish if Adam's love for her had been as great as hers for him, and she'd had to admit painfully that he'd loved the snow-clad peaks more than herself.

'I'm sorry, Helen,' Daniel said quickly. 'I shouldn't have reopened what must be a very painful subject. Forgive my curiosity and the criticism I was dishing out. It just seems insane that Kerwin should have jeopardised his marriage to a girl like you. He must have been a head case!'

Helen's face twisted. 'I had a rival, Daniel. Tall, white, exciting, and very beautiful.'

'You mean the mountains?'

'Yes. When he'd seduced one there was always another waiting.'

She was amazed how calm her voice sounded. . . amazed that she was telling this warm, vibrant stranger her innermost thoughts. Thoughts that she'd never expressed before out of loyalty to Adam, and most amazing of all was the fact that he understood.

But she was here to ask what he would like to drink. The children and Bruno had taken theirs outside and perhaps it was time they joined them, and so she said quickly, 'What can I get you? Whisky, wine, a beer perhaps?'

'A cup of tea would be most acceptable,' he said surprisingly.

'Tea? Yes, of course.' She was smiling 'It's clear that neither Bruno nor yourself intends being drunk in charge of a bicycle.'

He gave her his wide grin. 'Quite right. I mean, just supposing we were under the influence and steered into the lake — there's no guarantee that a delightful jogger would be in the vicinity.'

Helen eyed him warily. He surely didn't think her delightful after her abrupt behaviour to date?

'I would imagine that you're both capable of coping with most situations without assistance from the likes of myself,' she said drily.

'Bruno certainly is,' he agreed. 'He's an extremely capable lad, and the kids adore him. As for myself. . . yes. . . I *do* cope with most things, but there's one problem that absolutely floors me.'

'And what's that?' Helen asked.

'It's when they cry for their mother. I've no panacea for that.'

He'd said it matter-of-factly, in a flat, dead sort of way, but his face gave him away, the helpless misery in it, and Helen felt tears prick her eyelids. They'd both lost a partner through no fault of their own, it would seem, although as yet she knew no details of the death of Daniel's wife, but in his case it was worse because there were children involved, and, unless he married again, Thomas and Jonathan would be denied a woman's influence in their lives.

It was obvious that Daniel held the young German in

high regard, but it seemed strange that he'd chosen a man to care for his children.

He was waiting, watching her as if hoping she might have some magical solution to offer, but of course there wasn't one, was there? Her hand came out and she stroked the back of his wrist gently with long, slender fingers.

It was purely a gesture of compassion, but at her touch his hand swivelled over and grasped hers, and as he looked into her startled hazel eyes Daniel gave a smothered groan, and then as if unable to stop himself he pulled her into his arms and buried his face against the dark silk of her hair.

Helen stood quite still. It was a strange, timeless sort of moment. Totally unexpected. . .totally revealing, as he murmured, 'It's a long time since I held a lovely woman in my arms, Helen. I'd almost forgotten the pure joy of it.'

She came alive then. Her arms came up and she cradled him to her. She could feel the need in him. . . the longing for comfort, and she said softly, 'I haven't exactly been involved in many close encounters myself lately.'

He lifted his head at that, and, at the expression in his eyes, tenderness, longing, and a thousand other emotions swept through her.

'Is that so?' he whispered. 'What about "ginger nut" at the dance?'

Helen smiled. 'I told you. . .he's just a friend,' and then as sudden panic gripped her she thought, And you're just an acquaintance. What on earth am I thinking of? But his lips were seeking hers and she was too mesmerised to move her mouth.

It was just a butterfly kiss, light and fleeting, and

when he released her Daniel said wryly, 'I was forgetting that my sons are just a few yards away,' and as if to verify that fact they came charging back inside at that moment, and if Bruno, who was close behind, wondered why the big fair man who was his employer, and the beautiful young doctor who lived all alone, were standing so close he gave no sign.

Daniel never did get his cup of tea. Jonathan informed him that he'd got a puncture, and by the time his bike had been repaired the sun was setting over the lake and the children were yawning.

'I'm afraid we'll have to go, Helen,' he said. 'The boys are tired, and I'm expecting someone later. Can we put the cuppa on hold until another time?'

'Yes, of course,' she said easily. 'I've enjoyed your unexpected visit, and thanks again for the jogging suit. However did you manage to find an exact replica?'

He gave his deep, rumbling laugh. 'I asked your mother for details when we met on Saturday night, and Bruno is an excellent. . .'

'Shopper?' she said, flashing a smile at the tall German au pair.

'Got it in one,' Daniel said, and then to the boys, 'Say goodnight to Helen, you guys,' and once they had done so the all-male quartet prepared to move off.

He paused for a moment, one foot on the ground, hands loosely on the handlebars, and Helen thought that in the white cotton shirt and blue denim shorts he was wearing he looked cool and relaxed, and when he called breezily, 'Bye, then. See you tomorrow, Helen,' it was hard to believe she'd been in his arms just a short time ago. There was no sign of the misery and subsequent arousal that had taken place in her sitting-room, and she didn't know whether to be relieved or peeved.

When they set off Daniel was at the front, the boys in the middle, and Bruno peddling slowly at the back. After a few yards Bruno stopped and wheeled back to where Helen was still standing at the gate.

'What's wrong?' she asked.

'Nothing is wrong,' he told her with his engaging smile. 'I wish to speak with you alone.'

Helen frowned. 'Why?'

'It is my night off tomorrow, and as all my friends are in Germany and Australia I have no one to spend the time with. I wonder if you would let me take you somewhere? To dine perhaps. . .or a show. . .or both? It would please me to have your company.'

It was a polite and most unexpected invitation and she didn't know what to say. The night was full of surprises and here was another. She thought quickly. Short of being called out on an emergency she had nothing planned for the following night, and Bruno was an attractive and likeable young man, so. . .why not?

'That would be nice,' she said hurriedly, aware that his presence was likely to be missed any second, and the last thing she wanted was for Daniel Reed to think she was waylaying his staff. 'Shall *I* choose somewhere?' she suggested. 'I know the area much better than you.'

'Yes, please do. I will call for you at eight o'clock?'

Helen nodded. 'Fine.'

And then, as if his thoughts were in line with hers, he clamped his feet on the pedals and rode off at full speed.

'Whew!' In the sitting-room Helen sank down on to one of the chairs. What an evening! She had been the recipient of a thoughtful and unexpected gift, had opened her heart to a man that she wasn't even sure she liked, been in his arms, kissed by him fleetingly. . .and would have liked it to go on longer, if only to see if he could make her tick, and then finally had made a rather furtive assignation with a male au pair. What next?

James Deardon wouldn't like it if he knew she'd arranged to spend the evening with Bruno Hengist, but it was just too bad. He didn't own her, though he'd like to think he did. It was strange that both he and Bruno were attractive in their vastly different ways, but they didn't make her heart beat any faster. It was a man with a craggy thrown-together face and a deep fount of humour who did that, a man who had put her long grief over Adam into perspective in a matter of seconds, and she wasn't sure that she wanted it to be that way. The thing that mattered was they had to work together in St Margaret's; personal feelings shouldn't come into it. Relationships between hospital staff usually foundered with the strains and stresses of the job, and Helen had no wish to become another casualty, or so she told herself.

From the moment she'd jumped into the lake to rescue the delightful Thomas her life hadn't been the same, and for someone who liked order in all things it was disturbing to say the least.

Adam's photograph was facing her in its expensive wooden frame and she walked across and touched his face gently. 'I know you loved me, Adam,' she said softly, 'but I just couldn't compete with that other love, could I?'

Twice in one night she was admitting to herself the truth of what had happened all that time ago, and she felt cleansed and free because of it, and with a sudden lightness of heart, and skirts flying, Helen danced a happy jig around the room.

As she was on the point of going to bed the phone rang. It was her mother.

'Dad and I passed your place earlier,' Margaret said after they'd exchanged greetings, 'but we didn't call, as it looked as if you were entertaining the local cycling club.'

Helen laughed. 'It was Daniel Reed and his entourage. They'd brought me a replacement for the suit that went in the lake. I believe you knew about it?'

'Sort of,' her mother admitted. 'He was concerned that your clothes would have been ruined and asked me where he might get another suit like the one you were wearing. A charming man, I thought. . .and what does this entourage of his consist of?' she asked curiously.

'Two bonny little boys and a German au pair.'

'You're kidding!' Margaret exclaimed. 'No wife?'

'No. Daniel Reed's a widower.'

'Really? Well, I don't think that will be for long. A man as engaging as that will soon be back in harness.'

'Mother!' Helen protested. 'Every woman isn't after the first presentable male she meets.'

Margaret gave a wicked chuckle. 'Yes, I agree. *You* aren't, for one, but you have to admit there aren't many like you.'

Helen gave a dry laugh. 'It's perhaps as well or the birth-rate would fall dramatically.'

'Do we know what happened to his wife?' her mother was asking.

'No, *we* don't, and it really isn't the kind of question I'm going to be throwing at him on such short acquaintance, is it?'

'No, dear, of course not,' she agreed, 'and anyway, whatever Daniel Reed's private life holds, it will make a nice change for you working with someone like him instead of an elderly man.'

'Yes, it will, and please don't go getting any ideas about him. I'm going out with the au pair tomorrow night.'

'Is that so? Well, it's nice to have a night out with another woman, but don't you think you should be looking towards a more permanent. . .?'

Helen broke into her mother's well meant advice. 'The au pair is a stunning German *male* called Bruno Hengist.'

There was a surprised silence and then Margaret gave a low laugh. 'I think that your dad and I can stop worrying about you, daughter dear, what with Jim, this au pair person, *and* the charming widower.'

Helen had to laugh. 'The first two maybe, but Daniel Reed is merely a colleague. . .and a senior one at that.'

'Yes, of course, dear,' said her unrepentant parent.

The night was warm and humid, and in the early hours a storm broke. Helen, who had been tossing restlessly since going to bed, lay watching the jagged flashes in the sky before each thunderous roll, and hoped that it wasn't disturbing Thomas and Jonathan. She could hear the trees by the lake swaying in the warm wind and the water slapping anxiously against the stones, and she felt a sudden urge to go to them. . .to make sure they weren't crying for their mother, and, if they were, to cradle them in her arms. It was a crazy thought, of course, as they had a loving father there for them, and yet hadn't he told her it was the only time he couldn't cope? Yes, he had, but not as such that it would warrant her turning up in the middle of the night as a poor substitute.

She could phone to check. No, she couldn't. That

would be stupid. Helen looked at the clock. It said half-past one. Daniel Reed wouldn't thank her for ringing at this hour. If the children were asleep it might waken them, and then they really would be aware of the storm.

Helen sat up in bed. It would only take a matter of minutes to cross the park. If the house was in darkness and all quiet she could slip back home and no one would be the wiser. Although the elements were raging in the night sky the rain hadn't come as yet and it was light enough to see her way.

If Daniel's children hadn't been on her mind so much she might have hesitated, but she told herself there wasn't likely to be anyone in the park at that hour, and, if there was, the lessons she'd taken in self-defence when a student doctor on Casualty would come in handy.

Daniel's house *was* in darkness, and all *was* quiet as she surveyed it from the path that she had walked along on the day she'd pulled Thomas out of the lake. Helen felt more than a little foolish. She was behaving like a neurotic fusspot, she told herself. She always told the over-anxious parents of the children she treated to take it calmly, not to over-react, and here she was doing the same. If anyone saw her standing here in the middle of the storm that was even now starting to show signs of the deluge to come they would think she was crazy, and she turned to make a speedy return to the cottage.

'Bruno's room is on the side,' a voice said from near by, and Helen went weak with shock. 'That is if you're just arriving. On the other hand, if you're on the point of departure you'll already be aware of its location, and it's quite all right to use the front door, Helen. This place isn't a monastery. He's allowed visitors day or night as long as it doesn't affect the children.'

She was staring at him speechless. Only Daniel Reed could make the kind of offensive accusation he'd just made with such bland pleasantness.

'I take it that you and he have something going. I saw him drop behind when we left your place earlier. He's a good lad, Helen, none better. You make an attractive pair.'

Helen knew she should be denying it, telling him to go to hell. Did he honestly think she would creep into his house to make love with an employee under his very nose, and with his children sleeping near by?

'I came out to get a breath of air,' he was saying, 'and to watch the storm. I hadn't gone to bed as I wanted to be awake if it aroused either of the boys, though they've seen worse than this in Australia.'

After his assumptions regarding herself and Bruno there was no way Helen was going to tell him that she'd been concerned about them too, and, finding her voice at last she said coldly, 'I was about to explain what I'm doing here, but as you've already done it for me I'll save my breath. . .and bid you goodnight.'

'Just a minute.' He caught her arm. 'You're not going back through the park on your own. For one thing the heavens are about to open, and for another it isn't safe. I'm coming with you.'

Helen glared at him. 'You're not! I'm quite capable of getting home under my own steam, and furthermore you can't leave the children.'

He sighed. 'As we are both well aware, Bruno is in the house, and it will only be a matter of minutes. Just wait a second and I'll go and get an umbrella.'

The moment he had gone striding into the house Helen began to sprint back the way she had come, anger lending wings to her feet. How dared he treat her like some pushy nymphet, and then in the next breath give his condescending approval? How would he have reacted if he'd known the real reason for her appearance at his gates in the middle of a storm? Probably thought she was out of her mind, she decided bitterly.

By the time she got back to the cottage Helen was soaked; the opening of the heavens that had been threatening all the time she'd been out had manifested itself when she was halfway back and the rain had come down in torrents.

As she hurried into the bathroom to take off her wet clothes the phone rang and she didn't need two guesses as to who it might be.

'That was a bit stupid, wasn't it?' he said. 'You must be drenched.'

'Yes, I am,' she said flippantly, 'but what's a spot or two of rain? I'll soon dry out.'

'You're a head case to be out in the park at night on your own,' he said, and when there was no answer forthcoming, 'Do you hear me, Helen?'

'Yes, I hear you, Daniel,' she said wearily, 'and now, if you'll excuse me, I'm going to bed. I don't know what your list is like for Theatre tomorrow, but mine is quite long enough, and I don't want to be falling asleep on the job.'

'Have you locked up?'

Helen glowered at the receiver. Did he think her totally irresponsible? 'Of course I have!' she snapped. 'What do you think I am?'

She heard his deep chuckle at the other end of the line and almost choked with annoyance as he said, 'Earlier this evening I could have answered that straight off, but now I'm not so sure.'

Sliding between the sheets once more, Helen

thumped the pillows angrily. The memory of the lovely evening had been blotted out by the fiasco out there in the park. She was fuming at Daniel's insulting assumption that she'd been on a furtive visit to Bruno, but even more furious at his 'Bless you, my children' attitude.

A bit of annoyance or outrage wouldn't have come amiss, but that kind of reaction usually came from jealousy, or at the least more than a passing interest, and Daniel had made it quite clear there was nothing like that in his thoughts.

As Helen finally composed herself for sleep it was with the thought in *her* mind that there had been one good thing; the children had slept through the storm. It had passed over now and a full moon shone in a starlit sky, and the only turbulence remaining was inside herself.

CHAPTER FIVE

IN SPITE of her nocturnal wanderings Helen was awake early, but the sunlight slanting in through the latticed window of her bedroom and the birdsong outside seemed to have lost their magic this morning, and the reason wasn't hard to find.

Helen's first thought on opening her eyes was of the humiliating scene beside the lake, and her second was that if it was humanly possible while working in such close proximity she was going to steer clear of Daniel Reed.

She felt irritable and out of sorts as she made her way to St Margaret's, and when she walked into the staff-room those present eyed her warily.

'Hectic night, Helen?' Mike Norton asked with a grin.

'Yes, but not in the way you mean,' she said briefly.

'You weren't called out, were you?'

'No.'

'Well, then?'

Helen managed a smile. She liked the Lancashire lad. 'Give it a rest, will you, Mikey? I'm in Theatre in fifteen minutes. . .and *you're* with me, John,' she told his less exuberant companion.

'Yeah, and it's me for Outpatients,' Mike said dolefully. 'Our Jilly's assisting Danny Boy.'

'Is that so?' Helen couldn't have cared less. She'd seen enough of Daniel Reed last night to last a lifetime.

The tonsillectomy was first on her list, to be followed by assisting the plastic surgeon with the closing of a cleft

64

lip, and the rest were minor repairs that she would supervise as John performed them.

There was nothing too serious in the morning ahead, but momentous enough to the parents and children concerned, and because of that fact every item of surgery would have her meticulous attention.

Daniel would be dealing with the more specialised cases, and she'd seen that one of them was a Wilm's tumour. Helen would have liked to be in on it as she hadn't encountered it before, but if he didn't suggest it there was no way she was going to be there unasked, and in any case she didn't want to see him. . .did she?

The staff were gowned and waiting for him in the first theatre and as Helen passed the door music blared forth. She halted in her tracks, annoyance and amazement coursing through her. Hugh Copley had never allowed any distractions in Theatre, much to the annoyance of some of the junior officers, and Helen had agreed with his ruling, but his place had been taken by a totally different kind of man. Maybe Daniel liked a racket while he was working, but one thing was sure. . . *she* didn't.

'Switch that off!' she snapped. 'I'll never be able to concentrate with that in my ears!'

The theatre sister who had been tapping her feet in time to the music looked up from the tray of instruments she was checking. 'It's Mr Reed's radio. He likes music while he's operating.'

Helen's face tightened. 'I see. Well, if that's the case, why not bring on the clowns and performing seals, and make a proper circus of it?'

She was being unreasonable and bad-tempered. . . she knew it, but he really was the limit.

'One clown reporting for duty,' his voice said from

behind her, and as she whirled to face him Daniel said contritely, 'Yes, I *am* a clown, Helen. I got it all wrong last night, didn't I? Bruno told me this morning that he knew nothing of your visit last night. . .and he doesn't lie. Your being there wasn't anything to do with him, was it?'

'No,' she said stonily, hazel eyes flashing, 'it wasn't.'

'So what *were* you doing there in the middle of the night? It seemed a logical conclusion. . .you and he. . . free and unfettered. . .an attractive pair,' he said with a wry smile.

Helen thought he had the same look he'd had when he'd talked about the children missing their mother, a sort of lost, defeated expression, and she wondered what ailed him now. Would it perk him up if she told him she thought that Bruno was too young for her. . . because he was, and not due to any age-difference if there should be any, but because he *seemed* young, and there were times when *she* felt as old as Methuselah?

So now that his theory had been squashed Daniel wanted to know what she'd been doing outside his house in the middle of the night. She supposed *she* could indulge in a flight of fancy this time, or she could tell him the truth, and, though doing that was often the most embarrassing or uncomfortable thing to do in the first instance, it usually proved less painful in the end.

'I thought that the children might be woken by the storm and missing their mother,' she told him flatly. 'Sometimes a woman's presence can be. . .'

Daniel whistled softly. 'So that was it. I never dreamt——'

'That I would take it upon myself to poke my nose into your household arrangements,' she interrupted, 'but I assure you——'

It was Daniel's turn to cut *her* short. 'If the storm *had* disturbed them they would have loved a cuddle against soft, warm curves instead of my hard muscle. So would I, for that matter,' he said with a low chuckle that brought the colour up in her face.

Helen glared at him. He'd just generously admitted his mistake from the night before, and now he was spoiling it by being flippant.

'Yes, well, I'm sure you would get plenty of offers if you ask around,' she said levelly, 'and I'd be obliged if you'd turn the music down.'

He raised an amused eyebrow. 'Even if it should prove to be soothing and romantic?'

Helen was aware that they were being watched with interest by the theatre staff, and, still pink-cheeked, she hissed angrily, 'Why, no! If it should be that sort of music we wouldn't want to waste it, would we? A slow jive in the corridor between operations would be lovely!' And on that note she departed to do the thing she was best at. . .her job, knowing instinctively as she did so that in spite of his irritating ways Daniel Reed wouldn't be lacking in expertise either.

Philip Curtis had been seen in Outpatients regarding attacks of severe tonsillitis and quinsy, and had been referred for surgery. Today it was to be carried out, and as Helen looked down at the unconscious child she thought he would be even less enthusiastic about the operation when he awoke with a throat that felt like broken glass.

Hopefully a diet that included plenty of ice-cream might help to console him, and the assurance that the painful throat infections would be a thing of the past.

He had been anaesthetised and now Helen was able

to depress his tongue and, with blunt-nosed forceps in the one hand and a standard pair in the other, prise the tonsils away from the back of the throat and cut them away.

For twenty-four hours after the operation there would be bleeding in the throat, and once back in the ward Philip would be put on his side to avoid choking, and for the bleeding level to be detected.

If there was an excessive amount of pain in the throat and ears after the surgery it would be controlled with an analgesic drug, and as with the ice-cream a diet of soft foods and fluids would be introduced for the first few days. Operations for tonsil infections were not as frequent as in the past when surgery was almost invariably carried out on children with throat problems, but in a case like Philip's it was the obvious solution, and within two to three weeks the patient should have made a full recovery.

Baby James Brewster's problem was something totally different. At just three months old he had been brought into theatre to have a cleft lip closed, and as Helen examined him thoughtfully she recalled the horror of his parents when they had first seen his face.

'My baby looks awful, Doctor!' his pretty young mother had cried. 'I can't bear to look at him!'

The girl's boyfriend, a thin youth with apprehensive eyes, had said raggedly, 'He's ours, Donna, and he didn't ask to be born. We've got to help him all we can,' and when she'd nodded numbly he'd turned to Helen and said, 'Show us what to do, Doctor. How are we going to feed him?'

Helen and a nurse from the plastic surgery unit had done just that, and now at three months the cleft lip was to be closed, with Donna and her boyfriend anxiously awaiting the results of surgery that would give their little boy an improved appearance, and, more important than that, fewer feeding problems.

When she had brought the baby to Outpatients, Donna had told Helen, 'I'm ashamed of the way I behaved when he was born, Doctor. It was the shock. James is lovely. We both love him a lot, and if he isn't beautiful to anybody else he is to us.'

Helen had smiled. 'That's certainly the right way to look at it, Donna,' she'd said, 'and bear in mind the elastic strapping we've applied will help to lessen the cleft in James's lip. When he's three months old we'll have him in and the plastic surgeon will close it, and that should benefit him greatly.

'I think I've mentioned to you that it's fortunate that James has only a cleft lip. Sometimes the palate is cleft as well, and that makes everything, especially feeding, very difficult.'

The next bit had been hard to say, but it had to be said, and Helen had told the young mother gently, 'There is a risk of the same thing happening to any other children you might have, Donna. That's something you have to be aware of.' And as she'd looked into the girl's stricken face Helen had thought, as she'd done many times before, that nature played some sick jokes on mankind.

But today the promise she'd made that day in Outpatients was about to be kept. The plastic surgeon was going to draw together the two sides of the cleft, and Baby Brewster could only look better for it.

By the time John Travers had performed the two minor operations included in the timetable it was lunchtime, and as she changed out of her theatre clothes

Helen was aware that music was still issuing forth from the other room.

It would appear that Daniel was still operating, and she thought again that she would have liked to be present to assist with the removal of the nephroblastoma. The patient, Richard, a four-year-old, had been receiving radiotherapy and intravenous vincristine and actinomycin to reduce the size of the tumour, and now Daniel was to perform a right nephrectomy which would result in the loss of a kidney and with it the removal of the reduced tumour.

Wilm's tumour, as it was sometimes called, was a serious malignant illness of childhood, but hopefully after today the little boy's life expectancy would be vastly improved.

The music stopped, the door opened, and he was framed in it, smiling his easy smile.

'How did it go?' she asked quickly.

'Very well, Helen, but I'd have liked you in there with me. You missed the opportunity of being involved in a very interesting operation. I'm sure our worthy plastic surgeon could have coped with just young Travers to assist.'

'Why didn't you suggest it, then?' she said defensively. 'I wasn't going to come barging in uninvited. . . and I did have my morning arranged.'

'Arrangements can be altered,' he said mildly.

'Not unless absolutely necessary when it's messing about with children's lives,' she said evenly.

'Increasing our knowledge and experience is beneficial to the children we care for just as much as keeping to a strict schedule,' he pointed out.

'I don't think I need anyone to tell me that,' she said coldly, 'but nothing is achieved in chaos.'

He reached out and touched her smooth cheek gently. 'You're the most meticulous woman I've ever met, Helen. I must be a constant source of irritation to you.'

'Yes, you are.'

It had come out almost without thinking, but it was the truth, and he *had* brought the subject up, and yet in a half-hearted attempt at appeasement she was driven to say, 'I suppose that you find me just as irritating?'

His face sobered. 'No, I don't. I find you different from other women I've met, I'll admit that.'

Her heartbeat quickened. 'What do you mean by that?'

'You're the first woman I've met who's more interested in my children than me. It's usually the other way round. I get the warm welcome, but the kiddywinks are an encumbrance to be tolerated. *You* brought Thomas out of the lake, and were concerned about them during the storm.'

So Daniel didn't think she was interested in him. That was debatable. She'd just told him he irritated her. . . and he did. . .but the fact remained that from the moment of their meeting he'd never been out of her thoughts, and when he'd kissed her in her sitting-room last night she'd wanted it to go on. . .and on.

What he had just said had been revealing. He was admitting to success with her own sex, but was aware that every woman didn't want a ready-made family. A lump came up in her throat. Her life was full of children . . .sick children. . .and she loved them all, and it wouldn't be hard to love Thomas and Jonathan.

He was watching her. 'A penny for your thoughts?'

'They're worth a lot more than that, Daniel,' she said softly. 'I was thinking that. . .'

'Excuse me,' a voice said from behind him. 'You're

blocking the doorway, Mr Reed,' and as he stepped aside with an apologetic smile Jill Morrison said pertly, 'That was a very interesting morning. Thanks for having me.'

He grinned back at her. 'Any time, Jill.'

Helen flinched. She'd been on the point of making a fool of herself. She wasn't exactly sure how, but she'd felt herself mellowing towards him. There'd been a warmth inside her that had made her want to reach out to Daniel, but it had died as she watched his easy familiarity with Jill, and without any further conversation between them Helen turned swiftly and followed the blonde senior house officer down the corridor.

She saw Daniel for a brief second in the car park at the end of the day but there was no prolonged conversation between them this time. He merely waved and called, 'Must dash, it's Bruno's night off.'

Well, of course, she knew that, didn't she? And ever since she'd agreed to spend the evening with the au pair Helen had been having second thoughts, though she was blessed if she knew why. She was a free agent, and Bruno seemed nice enough, so why shouldn't she live a little? Was it because of Daniel's assumption the previous night that they 'had something going', as he'd put it? All right, it could make it rather embarrassing when he discovered they'd been out, but, as she'd just told herself, she *was* free to do as she pleased.

She didn't think he would disapprove if he did find out. He'd been at pains to make that clear last night. Within five minutes of assuming she was there to see Bruno he'd been ready to pat them on the head and give them his blessing! But there was no saying he wouldn't get a laugh out of being partly right, and Helen felt she could do without that.

Yet why on earth was she concerning herself about Daniel's reaction to her dating the young German? she asked herself as she swung her car out of the hospital gates and headed for home. It was more likely to be Jim Deardon who would have a sour face when he knew what she'd been up to, and she'd no need to be concerned about him either.

As she showered and changed for the evening ahead Helen had one last piece of advice for herself: Go out and enjoy yourself. Forget all about charismatic widowers with enchanting children. . .if you *can*.

When Bruno came loping down her path with his long stride Helen was ready and waiting, and he eyed her approvingly.

'You look very. . .swish, Helen,' he said.

She laughed and he immediately looked uncomfortable. 'Swish is not a good word?' he queried.

'Yes, of course, Bruno,' she reassured him. 'It's just that it's a slangy sort of expression that I wouldn't have expected you to know.'

'Oh, I see,' he said, relieved. 'I had heard Daniel say it, so I thought. . .'

'Yes, I imagine it's a word Daniel *would* use,' she said drily.

'He is the tease, my employer,' he said with a grin, confidence restored, 'but a great guy to work for.'

'I don't think I could disagree on either side of those comments,' Helen agreed in the same dry tone as she locked the door and deposited the key in her bag.

She was wearing a turquoise silk shift dress with a long gold chain and earrings to match. It was mini-skirted and showed off her long legs to advantage. Cream shoes and handbag made up the ensemble, and as she'd looked herself over on completing dressing

Helen had been satisfied with the result. If Bruno's warm, admiring gaze was anything to go by, so was he.

Helen had chosen an excellent but not too expensive restaurant in the town centre — a venue that would be appropriate if Bruno hadn't got transport, as she could drive them the short distance in her car without him feeling at a disadvantage.

It transpired that he hadn't. When she asked if he'd driven over he said, 'No. I walk the short way around the lake. I will get us taxi, huh?'

'No, don't do that,' Helen said quickly. 'I'll drive,' and as he was about to protest, 'It's only a short distance to the place I've chosen. We'll be there in a matter of minutes.'

The Old Steak House by the market-place was one of the town's best eating places and there were quite a few people already dining as they were shown to their table. Once they had ordered the food Bruno leant back in his chair and asked, 'And how was your day, Helen?'

'Busy as always,' she replied. 'I was in Theatre this morning, and it was Outpatients' clinic this afternoon. How was yours?'

She was curious about the household at the other side of the lake, and not just because it was Daniel Reed's. A paediatric surgeon, a German au pair and two motherless small boys was a strange mixture. Bruno in particular was such an unlikely choice for the position he held in it, and Helen was interested to know how it came about.

'Good. A good day it has been. This morning the boys play while I clean the house, and then after lunch we go into the park and watch them build the stage for the theatre.'

'But of course!' Helen exclaimed. 'There's to be an

open-air theatre in the park for the next week, isn't there? A marvellous idea as long as the weather holds. I shall most certainly go one evening.'

'Perhaps we could go together,' he suggested.

'Don't rush me, Bruno,' she protested laughingly. 'We've only just met. I hardly know you.'

'What is it that you would wish to know about me?' he asked.

'Why you're working as an au pair, for one thing? It seems such a strange job for a man.'

He smiled, showing the pearly white teeth again. 'It is only for the one year, Helen. In two months' time I move on.'

She gave a small gasp of dismay. 'Oh, dear! What about the children? Does Daniel know?'

'But of course. He understood it was only for a short time. It was an agreement between us. Daniel, he needed someone to be with Jonathan and Thomas while he is at the hospital, and I needed funds to cover the year before I go to college.'

'Why you, though?' she asked curiously. 'Did you already know each other?'

'Yes. I was the tennis coach at the Racket Club in Sydney, where Marianne, his wife, was the star player. She always brought the children with her and we were all very friendly. Also I am the eldest of a large family and am used to looking after little ones. So when she died I did what I could for them.'

'Was it an accident?' Helen asked carefully.

'No. It was not an accident. On a very hot day Marianne had been on the courts for most of the afternoon when she suddenly collapsed. It was the heart. . .very quick, very final. There was nothing to be done.'

'And Daniel. . .where was he?'

'Working, at the hospital. He accepted it better than most; after all, he is the doctor. But they were hard days for him and the children. He had already decided to come back to England, and Marianne was happy to come with him, even though it meant leaving her own country. So when the time came for him to take up his appointment here I came along with them. I call myself the au pair but I'm not really. It's just a matter of my being there for the children and Daniel. He can leave them with me with ease of mind when he goes to the hospital, and while he is away I do chores around the house for which he pays me. It would be hard for him if I weren't here.'

'Yes, of course,' she murmured as the vision of their first meeting came into her mind. She could see him tired and crumpled, stretched out on the settee, and hear the soft plop of the water dripping off her clothes, and remember her embarrassment when she'd discovered that he'd been at St Margaret's all night instead of carousing.

She wished suddenly that it were *he* sitting across the table from her instead of the likeable German youth, so that she could tell him how sorry she was for the pain he had suffered, and tell him that she hoped he would find someone just as kind as Bruno to take over when he left. But, knowing Daniel, he would probably just laugh and shrug off her concern and she'd be left squirming.

By the time they had finished eating it was too late to catch a show, and so they strolled around the town, along the elegant shopping promenade with its imposing Georgian façade, and past the Spa Pavilion, white-domed among emerald lawns.

As the sun began to set in a clear summer sky Bruno

pointed to a small wine-bar in a tree-lined square. 'Would you like a drink, Helen?' he asked.

'Yes, why not?' she agreed. 'But orange juice for me, please, as I'm driving.'

At half-past ten Helen picked up her bag and got to her feet. 'I think it's time we made tracks,' she said. 'I don't want a late night, Bruno. I have to be at St Margaret's bright and early in the morning, and I'm sure *you* don't get the chance to lie in very often with Jonathan and Thomas around.'

He stood up reluctantly. 'Sure, if that's what you, want, Helen. It seems a waste, though. The night is young.'

'So are we,' she said wryly, 'and, if we want to stay that way, hitting the town until all hours isn't going to help.'

'You didn't mind being out late last night, though?' he questioned as they walked back to the car. 'Daniel said you were in the park past midnight, *and* with a storm overhead.'

'Yes, I was,' she admitted, 'but there seemed to be a very good reason for it at the time.'

'It was Daniel, wasn't it? He thought you were seeking me, but you'd come to see him, hadn't you? I've seen the way he looks at you, and you must have seen it too.'

Helen stopped in her tracks and turned to face him. She didn't know whether to be angry or amused. Daniel had thought she had a tryst with Bruno, and the young German thought that it was his employer she'd come to see, and they were both wrong.

'I didn't come out in the middle of the storm to see either of you,' she told him. 'I was concerned about the children; that they might be afraid.'

It was his turn to be surprised. 'But their father and I were both there for them.'

'I'm aware of that,' she told him steadily, 'and I realised afterwards it was a rather stupid thing to do. It was just that I thought they might be missing their mother, but I had a wasted journey, and got drenched going back through the park.'

'I guess you had a grand view of the storm, though.'

'Yes, I did, but it was a bit too close for comfort.'

She noticed he'd shown no concern for her safety. It took Daniel to do that.

When Helen stopped the car at the bottom of the drive to Daniel's house Bruno whispered her name softly, and as she turned towards him his arm slid along the back of the seat. Helen knew he was going to kiss her, and that she was going to let him. Hadn't Daniel been at pains to point out that he wasn't in charge of a monastery? Well, she wasn't convent bound either.

His lips were firm and eager. . .very eager, and after responding for the first few seconds Helen pushed him back with a shaky laugh. 'That's enough, Bruno,' she gasped. 'A goodnight kiss in this country is exactly that. We don't make a meal of it.'

He drew back with an angry little snort. 'I am sorry. Right moment. . .wrong man?'

'Don't jump to conclusions,' she said coolly, with the feeling inside her that he might be right.

'Conclusions?' He was questioning the meaning of the word.

'Yes, thoughts, ideas, and in this instance the wrong ones.'

He was smiling again. 'I see. So I am not the wrong man?'

'I didn't say that.'

He sighed. 'I am not sure that I am understanding. Maybe you will explain when we go to the theatre?'

'I didn't say we were going to the theatre either,' Helen told him exasperatedly, and as he got out of the car and stood looking down on her she said firmly, 'Goodnight, Bruno. It's been a pleasant evening,' and without giving him the chance to hold a post-mortem on that remark she was away.

CHAPTER SIX

IN THE end Helen went to the open-air theatre with Jim Deardon. He came round to the cottage the night after she'd been out with Bruno, and after a brusque greeting said, 'One of my patients saw you dining out last night with a blond guy. Who was he?'

Helen had only just finished her meal and had been sitting beside the window watching the wild ducks wheeling and swooping overhead, her mind only half on them as it went over the day she'd just spent at St Margaret's.

It was a day in which she'd seen little of Daniel. Everywhere she'd gone he'd just left, and instead of being pleased to be spared his irritating presence she'd felt frustrated and on edge.

The only time they'd exchanged words had been for a brief moment outside Pinocchio Ward when he'd said with a rather frayed smile, 'I hear you were a big hit with Bruno.'

She stifled a groan. So the au pair had told him they'd spent the evening together. Well, she'd known there was every chance he might. What of it? Nothing, except that she had a sudden urge to tell Daniel that Bruno hadn't been a big hit with *her*, but instead, causing him to stare at her in surprise, she'd asked, 'What's wrong, Daniel? Are you tired?'

'A bit,' he'd admitted. 'Thomas had a restless night, and when I'd finally got him settled I couldn't get to sleep myself, and I ended up in the kitchen drinking coffee in the company of your boyfriend.'

Helen's face had flamed. 'I told Bruno not to make assumptions and now you're doing the same. We just went for a meal, that's all,' she snapped.

'But of course! I'm forgetting. There's "ginger nut" in the running too, isn't there? What a full life you lead, Helen.' And he'd gone striding off, leaving her fuming.

And now the man in question was glowering at her and asking who was her companion of the previous night.

'His name is Bruno Hengist. He's an au pair,' Helen told him briefly, and was rewarded by the look of amazement on his face.

'An au pair! And a German one at that!' he spluttered.

'Got it in one, James,' she told him.

'Where did you meet him?'

'In the park. He looks after Daniel Reed's children.'

'Oh. I see.' For once the articulate Jim was short on words and Helen had to smile. 'And are you likely to be seeing him again?' he asked grittily.

'I don't know. Possibly not.'

His face lightened and Helen thought grimly that there was no way she was going to spend the rest of her life placating James. 'I suppose if it was just a one-off it doesn't matter,' he said magnanimously, and then in the next breath, 'I've got two tickets for Saturday, the first night of the open-air theatre in the park. Do you fancy coming?'

Helen hesitated. She'd intended going. . .but alone, and she thought how strange it was that she'd spent the last few years hurting inside, shutting herself off from relationships with the opposite sex, in a state of self-imposed celibacy, and now suddenly she was in demand, and it was disconcerting to say the least.

Three attractive men had come into her life, all of them unattached, and so far there'd been little joy in it. She'd found Bruno to be immature and too intense, the dynamic James too possessive, and Daniel. . .well, he irritated her, didn't he?

Yes, he did, but he intrigued her too, so much so that he was rarely out of her thoughts. Maybe it was because they'd both lost someone they loved, and in her case Helen had withdrawn into herself, while Daniel was just the opposite, a breezy extrovert. . .a charmer. . .easygoing and relaxed, except for the occasional glimpses of a less happy man.

James was persisting. 'I asked if you would come to the theatre with me. Remember?'

'Yes, of course. My mind was elsewhere,' she said slowly. 'That would be very nice. What's the show?'

'*The Song of Hiawatha*,' he said with a doubtful glance.

Helen's face lit up. 'Really? How lovely!' And then, 'That explains it, of course.'

'Explains what?'

'When I passed the other day they were erecting the stage and I wondered why they were building it virtually over the water on wooden supports, but for that type of production the setting on the lake will be ideal.'

'Good, then,' he said, gratified. 'I thought you might have preferred something more sophisticated.'

'No, certainly not. I've always loved *Hiawatha*. The words are beautiful.'

'It's a touring company from up north. They're doing it for three weeks, and then a following three weeks of *Winnie-the-Pooh* for the children,' he explained.

'Sounds great,' she said, aware that her enthusiasm was entirely for the show rather than the company of the man beside her.

Helen walked into the staffroom on Thursday morning to find Mike Norton and Jill Morrison engaged in half-serious banter, and at her look of enquiry the young Lancastrian said with a grin, 'I've just wagered five pounds that our Jilly here won't be able to persuade Danny Boy to take her to the first night of the theatre in the park.'

'And I've told him he can wave goodbye to his fiver,' Jill said with a triumphant glance at Helen.

'So you're quite confident, then?' Helen asked with a smile that felt tight on her mouth.

Jill's answering smile had a complacency about it, the complacency of a woman who knew she was attractive to men. 'Quite. We have a lot in common, Daniel and I.'

Mike hooted with laughter. 'You mean medicine? Or the other thing that we all know about but never have time for. . .sex?'

Jill glared at him. 'Both!' and she marched out of the room.

'It's obvious that madam hasn't seen Reed's au pair,' John said with a chuckle. 'He's the original golden boy. Our laughing widower wouldn't stand a chance if she'd seen the German.'

Mike stared at him. 'That's the first I've heard of him. Did *you* know that Reed had a German au pair, Helen?'

'Yes,' she said shortly, shrugging into her ward coat. 'I'll see you boys later.'

As Helen passed the door of Pluto Ward Jalal was moving slowly and painfully towards the showers, but when he saw her he gave a cheerful wave, and as she waved back she almost collided with Daniel.

'Whoops!' His hand came out to steady her and as his fingers closed on her wrist the depression she'd felt during the flippant conversation in the staffroom disappeared.

Helen found herself looking down at the supple fingers that encircled her wrist as he had made no attempt to move them, and she was aware that the sudden contact, impersonal though it might be, was making her blood race.

The amazing blue eyes were laughing into hers, the wide mouth curving into the smile that she was beginning to know so well, and for a second she felt the most fantastic sensation of well-being, and then she spoilt it by asking stupidly, 'Have you seen Jill?'

He raised a questioning eyebrow. 'She of the come-hither eyes? No, I haven't. Should I have?'

'No. Not specially. I just wondered.'

'Huh? I don't get what you mean. Wondered what?'

Helen wriggled out of his grasp. 'It was nothing. I was just questioning if she'd come on duty yet.'

'Oh, I see. Well, I don't know about Morrison, but the moment that *I* walked into the building there was a call for me to go down to Maternity. A tiny mite with Talipes. Both feet are in-turned from the ankle and the houseman isn't having any joy in being able to even partially correct the problem. It's a pretty bad case and I'm not sure that exercise or plaster casts will put them right in the long run. Only time will tell, but I feel it may end up in the tendons having to be lengthened at some future date.

'And by the way, the kid with anorexia is playing the staff up this morning. Both parents came to see her last night. According to Sister they usually come separately, but the idiots came together to tell the poor little sausage that they're splitting up.'

'Oh, no!' Helen exclaimed in dismay. 'How selfish can you get? I'll go and have a word with her.'

'Yes, do that,' he agreed, 'and in the meantime I'll see how the rest of my dolly mixtures are getting on. Young Richard, the nephroblastoma, has had a bad couple of days, and I've had two frantic parents haunting me, but he's making good progress now, and if no further complications arise should have a future, which he didn't have before.'

Joanne was huddled beneath the bedclothes when Helen went to see her. 'Hasn't eaten a thing this morning,' a young nurse who was hovering near by told her. 'Says she wants to die.'

Helen pulled the sheets back and looked at the too thin child curled foetus-like on the bed. 'Joanne,' she said softly, 'aren't you going to have some breakfast?'

'No,' she mumbled, turning her face away.

Helen took the bull by the horns. 'You're upset about your mum and dad splitting up, aren't you?' she asked gently.

There was no answer.

'Do you know what I'd do if I were you?' Joanne shook her head in slow misery. 'I'd show them that if they want to behave childishly you're not going to do the same, and that you're not going to make yourself ill because of them,' Helen said.

The young girl hunched her shoulders higher and kicked out aimlessly with a thin leg, but she didn't speak.

'Which of them would you prefer to live with?' Helen asked. 'Have either of them suggested it?'

'They both want me. . .but *I* don't want *them*,' she whispered.

'Then who *would* you like to live with?'

Joanne turned her head a fraction and one dark eye looked up at the concerned registrar. 'You. I'd like to live with you, and if I can't then my granny May.'

'Me?' Helen asked in amazement. 'Why me, Joanne?'

''Cos I like you,' she gulped, 'and you haven't got anybody, have you?'

Helen felt a tight little pain around her heart. This child had hit right at a sore spot. No, she hadn't got anybody. . .no husband. . .no child. . .but she had two loving parents, which was more than this poor child had.

'I can't take you to live with me, Joanne,' she said softly, 'not when you have a family of your own. I'm sure that your parents wouldn't agree, but once you're out of here we can be friends. You can come to stay with me sometimes as my guest. I'd like that. Would you?'

Joanne almost managed a smile. 'Yes.'

'And so tell me about Granny May?' Helen coaxed.

'Joanne wants to go to live with her maternal grandmother,' Helen told Daniel later in the day, 'and I feel that her eating problems would disappear if that could be arranged.'

'You do? Well, that's a job for the hospital social worker, I would think, but if the parents are brought in for discussion I don't see why we can't be in on it. After all, I'm told that *you* were first choice,' he said with a smile. 'Sister overheard your little chat.'

'Yes, I was,' she said uncomfortably, 'and it was difficult to refuse the mixed-up child, but, as I explained to Joanne, she already has a family and I don't think they'd want her living with a stranger, and my work here is very demanding. . .'

'I agree with all you've said,' he told her, 'but isn't it nice to be so much in demand? My two rascals were asking this morning when they're going to see you again.'

Her beautiful hazel eyes widened. 'Really?'

'Yes. So what should I tell them?' he asked blandly.

'That I'll take them to see *Winnie-the-Pooh* if they like.'

'We could all go. How about that?' he suggested with a wicked twinkle in his eyes.

In that moment Helen knew that Daniel didn't irritate her any more. In fact she couldn't remember anything giving her so much pleasure before as the suggestion he'd just made, but she didn't intend capitulating so easily, and so she said casually, 'Yes, why not. As long as neither of us is on call.'

A shadow of disappointment crossed his face and Helen wished she'd shown more enthusiasm, but it was gone in an instant and he got up from the seat behind the desk in his consulting suite and came towards her. He put his hands on her shoulders and, his lived-in face only inches away from hers, he said softly, 'The girl Joanne is no fool. She sees that there is a very soft core beneath your crisp, meticulous exterior, and I'm aware of it too, Helen.'

'You are?' she breathed. 'You don't think I'm stiff and starchy?'

Laughter rumbled softly in his throat. 'Let's say that I can tell you don't always approve of me, but I'm thick-skinned as a rhinoceros, and the most optimistic of men.'

He was bending his head and his dazzling blue gaze

was so near she was drowning in it. There was a heat inside her that was making her feel weak and light-headed, because any second Daniel was going to kiss her, and this time she knew there would be no ending to it. It would be the beginning of something that, once started, would never finish.

When the phone on the desk beside him began to ring he pushed it away, but the spell was broken, and as he picked it up with a smothered groan his face tightened. He listened gravely for a moment and then said curtly, 'We'll be right there.'

Helen was leaning weakly against the desk trying to gather her wits, aware that the moment they'd just lost might never come again, as he said briskly, 'We're needed in Theatre, it would seem. A minibus taking children to the baths has crashed and they're transfer-ring some of them here from Casualty at the infirmary.'

There had been a dozen children in the mini-van and the accident had occurred because the elderly driver had suffered a stroke while taking them to the swimming-baths.

The infirmary had admitted the driver and six of the children with various types of fractures. Out of the remainder three were severely shocked but unhurt, and the others had received head injuries.

Seven new admissions were about as much as the bed availability at the infirmary could offer, and so the others had been switched to St Margaret's.

There was a young teacher pacing the corridor when Helen and Daniel went to see what the initial examin-ation by the junior house officers had revealed. He was ashen-faced and trembling but still very much in control.

'You've got three twelve-year-olds in there,' he said, 'first-year pupils from Rossiter Comprehensive.' He swallowed hard. 'I was escorting them to the baths and. . .well, you know what happened. They were thrown about the coach like corks in a bottle.'

'Rossiter School!' Helen exclaimed. 'My mother is the headmistress there. She'll be frantic when she hears about this.'

'Margaret Blake?' the young man questioned. 'She knows already and is on her way to the infirmary now, and will no doubt come on here afterwards.'

There were two boys and a girl, their smart green uniforms torn and bloodstained, and Jill Morrison looked up as they approached. 'The girl seems to be the worst,' she announced. 'All three seem to have had nasty cracks on the head, but *she* was semi-conscious when brought in. We've had the skull X-rayed and there is a fracture of the occipital bone.'

As Daniel bent over the injured girl and felt gently around a deep gash on the temple her arms and legs moved jerkily but she didn't become aware, and as she went to inspect the other two Helen heard him give instructions for her to be placed in Intensive Care. 'Any signs of intracranial pressure and I want to know, OK, Jill?' he said.

'We were all sitting at the front, Doctor,' one of the boys said as Helen felt the huge bump that was coming up on his temple, 'an' when Mr Hodges collapsed the bus went on to the pavement and hit a wall.' He nodded towards his friend who was just being taken to X-ray. 'Jonesy and I were slammed up against the back of the driver's seat, but Sharon hit her head on the metal post between the seats. Next thing we knew we were all on the floor with those who'd been sitting behind on top of us.'

'I see,' Helen said gently. 'And were any of you,

apart from Sharon who is still semi-conscious, knocked senseless?'

'Jonesy was,' the amazingly composed lad told her. 'He was out for about ten minutes, but I wasn't. I didn't miss a thing, but it was scary, Doctor.'

'Yes, I'm sure it was, but from the sound of it things could have been a lot worse. Luckily no one was on the pavement at that particular moment. And now it's your turn for X-ray,' she told him as the porter approached with an empty trolley, 'but before you go one of the nurses will clean the nasty cut on your leg.'

As she moved away Daniel was at her side. 'We'll keep the two lads in overnight, Helen,' he said. 'Obviously the X-ray results will be our best guide, but even if they show no cause for alarm it's advisable we keep our eye on them for twenty-four hours. The girl is a different matter. She'll need watching. Did I hear the young fellow outside say they were from your mother's school?'

'Yes. Mum will be out of her mind. Thank God there were no fatalities. The infirmary say that none of the children's injuries is too serious, and that poor old George Hodges is holding his own in Intensive Care.'

'There are a lot of older men driving these days who should have check-ups regularly,' Daniel said. 'They do voluntary work or part-time jobs, and no one, including themselves, bothers to make sure they're fit enough to be on the road. Young lives were put at risk by what happened this morning.'

Helen nodded sombrely. He was right. Who knew better than those involved in health care of the carnage from the roads?

'That extremely lucid young boy says his friend was unconscious for a few minutes at the time of the crash,' she said. 'I'll tell Sister to keep her eye on him.'

She could hear her mother's voice, and when she went out on to the corridor Margaret was conversing anxiously with the young male teacher. When she caught sight of her daughter her face lightened a little, but there was no mistaking her distress.

'Next to the last day of term,' she said tightly. 'One more day and they all would have been on their summer holiday, and now we've got injured pupils in two hospitals.'

'That's true,' Helen said gently, 'but there were no fatalities. Be glad of that.'

'Yes, I suppose I must,' Margaret muttered. 'How are the three that were brought here?'

'The girl Sharon has a fracture of the occipital bone.'

'Where's that?'

'At the base of the skull. . .at the back, and one of the boys — I believe his name is Jones — was unconscious for a short period and is severely shocked. The third member of the trio is a very self-contained young man who doesn't seem to be too bad at the moment.'

'That'll be Anthony Green,' Margaret said. 'He's invariably the spokesman in any situation.' She ran her hand worriedly through her hair. 'We'll have parents arriving any moment. We've contacted as many as we can. This really is dreadful.'

'Yes, it is, Mum,' Helen agreed, 'but these things happen, and I'm going to organise a cup of hot, sweet tea for you and that young teacher over there, or we're going to have two more patients.'

In the midst of getting the children hospitalised and giving her mother what assistance she could there was little time to talk to Daniel, and when in the late afternoon he announced he was going to the infirmary to advise on treatment for one of the accident victims she knew that the special moment they'd shared in his office earlier in the day was receding rapidly.

As if tuned in to her thoughts again, Daniel paused on the brink of departure and said with a lop-sided grin, 'Aren't you glad to have been saved from a fate worse than death?'

Helen's face paled. Why did he have to make a joke out of everything? She was tempted to tell him that *he* was bringing her back to *life*, and if the promise of those moments earlier had been kept it could have been life most joyful, but she wasn't going to risk ridicule, and so with the grimace of a smile she said, 'Yes, aren't I the lucky one?'

The two boys from Rossiter Comprehensive had both had a stable night, but Sharon's condition had worsened. There had been a deterioration of the level of consciousness, and on the assumption that she had raised intracranial pressure she had been ventilated to reduce cerebral blood-flow and given mannitol.

Daniel had arranged an immediate CT brain scan, but fortunately there were no signs of a major bleed and he had ordered the treatment already being given to be continued.

Margaret Blake called in the middle of the morning, having first been to check on the patients at the infirmary. She reported that the driver was still in Intensive Care, and that the rest of them were progressing favourably, but there was consternation when she heard of Sharon's set-back.

'It's not as serious as it sounds,' Helen reassured her. 'There is no sign of a major bleed and she should settle down as the day goes on.'

CHAPTER SEVEN

As HELEN dressed for her date with James on Saturday she wondered if Jill had won the wager with Mike Norton. Would the pretty young doctor be at the theatre with Daniel?

Jill was a very determined young woman and very sure of her sexuality, and Daniel was only human. Hadn't he admitted here in her house that it was a long time since he'd held a woman? Maybe any attractive woman would do. Lots of men were like that, and as James came striding up her path in the mellow evening Helen thought she'd hate Daniel to be like that, but she wouldn't mind if it applied to the man approaching. In fact it would be a relief if his attention were directed elsewhere. His single-minded pursuit of her was a nuisance at times.

The setting sun glowed amber on the still waters of the lake as they walked across the park to the theatre complex, and Helen thought with a sudden melancholy that a golden night such as this should be spent with that special someone, the one who made all others seem insignificant. But one had to find the person first, and if she started asking herself if that had already happened she wasn't sure she could cope with the answer.

'You're very pensive,' James said as he draped his arm across her shoulders. 'Anything wrong?'

Her smile was strained. 'No. I was just wool-gathering.'

'Thanks a bunch!' he said with a brittle laugh. 'It's

days since we've seen each other and within the first few
minutes of being together again you're miles away. It's
not that au pair fellow, is it?'

Helen swung round on him, eyes flashing. 'No, it's
not, James, and if you want us to spend a pleasant
evening stop griping at me!'

His scowl deepened. 'I don't understand you, Helen.
Why are you so determined to keep me at arm's length?'

'I'm not aware of it,' she protested, knowing it wasn't
strictly true, 'but don't let's argue or the night will be
spoilt.'

James's face became less hard. 'All right, you win. A
truce it is,' and he gave her a quick, hard squeeze.

Helen steeled herself not to recoil, and at the same
time she was vowing this was the last occasion she was
going out with someone who meant nothing to her.

As they took their seats in the theatre area she looked
around her with pleasure. The stage was erected at the
other side of the narrow end of the lake so that a
glittering stretch of floodlit water separated it from the
audience. The seating was made from long lengths of
wooden planking set on a raised incline, and already it
was mostly occupied.

'I'm looking forward to this, James,' Helen told him,
eyes sparkling, their earlier exchange forgotten.

'Good. Will my genius in bringing you here be
suitably rewarded afterwards?' he asked with a meaningful smile.

Helen turned her head away. If ever awards were
given for insensitivity Jim Deardon should be on the list,
she thought wryly. Did he think she couldn't have
managed this on her own? That was what she'd intended
in the first place. And was he expecting the big bedroom
scene afterwards? He was due for a disappointment if

he was. She wasn't a prude, far from it, but after waiting all this time she wasn't going to give her body as a casual offering in a one-night stand or brief affair.

'If you mean can you come in for a coffee, by all means,' she said sweetly. 'I might even rise to a biscuit, but that will be all I'm offering. . .take it or leave it.'

Although the light was beginning to fade it was still clear enough to pick out faces, and as Helen's eyes went over the crowd she wondered if Jill Morrison *had* won the wager.

The answer came right on the heels of the thought. A group of young trendies were making their way down the centre passage between the seating, laughing and jostling between themselves, and among them, head and shoulders above the rest, and looking somewhat out of place, was a big fair-haired man.

In the instant that Helen recognised Daniel she also identified the young blonde close by his side, and with a sinking heart she thought that Jill knew her stuff.

At that moment the stage became floodlit, illuminating the waters of the lake and throwing the seating area into shadow. Try as she would Helen couldn't see where they had placed themselves, and as the strains of a haunting pagan overture came over the loudspeakers she brought her mind away from the foibles of Daniel Reed and prepared to enjoy the show.

The programme indicated that there would be two acts with three scenes in each. As the first scene unfolded above the glittering lake, the daughter of the moon, Nokomis, was jolted off her swing of grapevines in the sky and landed in a blossom-filled meadow to bear her first child, and as Helen watched she was transported to second-year English lit. and the magic of Longfellow.

The fact that James was fidgeting beside her barely registered as the lithe brown figures on the stage above the lake played their parts, and when Hiawatha and the other young braves paddled their canoes across the floodlit water the nostalgic beauty of the scene had her enthralled.

As the interval drew near and the wedding of Hiawatha and Laughing Water was enacted, with the soaring tenor voice of Chibiabos singing the beautiful aria 'Onaway! Awake Beloved!', James blew his nose loudly and broke the spell and Helen, on the edge of her seat drinking in the music, turned to him in exasperation.

'James!' she protested. 'What's wrong? Aren't you enjoying it?'

'No,' he muttered. 'I'm not. This airy-fairy stuff's not in my line. I wouldn't have brought you here if I'd known it would be all this sort of mumbo-jumbo.'

'You're the limit,' she spat angrily. 'Just because *you* don't like it there's no reason to spoil it for *me*.'

He got to his feet. 'I'm wasting my time with you, aren't I, Helen?' he snapped back. 'You don't really want to be with me, do you?'

'No, I don't!' she was stung to say.

'That settles it, then. I'm off!' and he pushed his way to the end of the seating and stamped off into the night.

When he had gone she thought that the anger inside her was as much at herself as at him. Doctor he might be, her father's partner he might be, but he was an insensitive, ignorant clod, and she should have given him his marching orders long ago.

She was almost tempted to leave the theatre herself. The spell of *Hiawatha* had been broken, and she too left her seat, but loath to go back to the empty cottage,

Helen went to stand by the fence that divided the seating from the rest of the park, and as she struggled to recapture the thrall of the scene across the water she realised that she wasn't alone.

'What's wrong, Helen?' Daniel's voice said quietly from behind her, 'I saw you leave your seat.'

She swung round in surprise. They must have been observing each other, but she'd lost track of *him* after those first few seconds.

'It's James. He's a pain,' she said tightly. '*Hiawatha* is too memorable to be spoilt by his boredom. We had a few words and he's gone off in a paddy.'

He smiled in the darkness. 'I see. I have to agree with you. Longfellow's poem is a verbal feast. "As unto the bow the cord is",' he quoted softly, '"So unto the man is woman; Though she bends him, she obeys him, Though she draws him, yet she follows; Useless each without the other."'

The timeless words hung between them and Helen's eyes were moist. He understood. The dolly-mixture doctor's mind was in tune with her. Did he feel, as she was beginning to, that there might be a time when *they* would be useless each without the other?

She'd felt a frail bond between them before, gossamer-fine, and in this enchanted moment it was strengthening into a lifeline that was fusing their minds, and setting her body on fire, taking the chill from her heart. With a clarity that almost took her breath away Helen saw that the one special person she'd been waiting for was here beside her, and it wasn't the magic of *Hiawatha* that was telling her that, it was the look in Daniel's eyes. They weren't even touching, and yet it was as if the vibrant warmth of him was wrapped around her in a secure embrace.

He laughed and the spell was broken. 'Water seems to be a ruling force in our lives. The first time I saw you was when you were dripping all over my carpet covered in pond-weed, and now here we are by the "Big-Sea-Water".'

Helen brought her mind back from tender pathways and answered him with the same kind of flippancy. 'Yes, and I know which I prefer.'

At that moment the lights around the enclosure came on for the interval.

'Do you want a drink, or shall we stroll around the park until the second act starts?' he asked.

Her heart lifted. He was intending they should stay together. 'Let's just stroll,' she said. 'There'll be a huge queue at the bars and for soft drinks.'

And so they did, through the scented gardens, by the silent playgrounds and empty tennis courts, until the lights went off again for the second half.

Daniel grabbed her hand and, swinging her round to face him, he laughed, 'Race you back to the theatre.'

'You're on!' she cried, and, giving him a playful push backwards, she was off, skirts flying, high heels sticking to the soft path. He was catching up easily and she wanted him to; after the revelation of her feelings for him Helen could hardly bear to take her eyes off him.

She stopped suddenly. 'What's the matter?' he breathed.

'It's James,' she whispered, 'just ahead of us. . . leaving the park.'

'Good,' he said with satisfaction. '*I'll* see you home safely.'

'What about Jill?' she questioned. 'You came here with her. I saw you. You can't just walk off and leave her. How will *she* get home?'

He gave an exasperated laugh. 'Jill again! What is it with you that you're always on about her? I didn't come with Jill. We arrived simultaneously and I got caught up in her crowd. I don't know whether it was planned, but to be quite truthful I don't think she'd be any more into *Hiawatha* than the departing James. No,' he gave her arm a gentle squeeze, 'I think out of the four of us I got the best deal.'

We both did, she thought happily as they settled themselves into a couple of empty seats.

When the show was over they walked back to the cottage. The park had emptied and only the great silver moon in the sky was there to see them. Bemused by *Hiawatha*, and doubly so by the man at her side, Helen was thinking of how she'd set out with James and was returning with Daniel.

She'd wished she could spend the evening with some-one special instead of James, never dreaming the fates would grant her wish, and so conveniently that she might have been uneasy if she'd been less happy.

At her gate they faced each other and he said softly, 'Goodnight, Minnehaha,' and took her hand in his. The romantic farewell and his touch brought a low laugh of pleasure from inside her. She felt happy, seductive, excited, and nervous all at once, and, not wanting the night to end, she said, 'Would you like to come in for a coffee?'

'I can't,' he said ruefully. 'Bruno's under the weather. He pulled a ligament in his leg this afternoon and the poor lad can hardly walk. *I* put the boys to bed, but if they should awake it could be difficult, and. . .' he gave a deep rumbling laugh '. . .I might get too comfortable in your cosy little nest. But I think there's one pleasure I could allow myself, Helen,' he said, his voice deepening.

'And what's that?' she asked breathlessly.

'I think you know,' he murmured as he released her hand and put his arms around her slender shoulders. There was no laughter in him now, just a gentle gravity in the deep blue eyes, and as she glowed back at him he said, 'The next time I see you all crisp and cool beneath your registrar's mantle I shall think I dreamt all this, but it's the most enjoyable way I know of thanking you for a memorable evening.'

As his mouth sought hers she murmured, 'Surely it's Longfellow you should be thanking.'

He was shaking his head in disagreement as he kissed her, and as she melted beneath his lips Helen was trying to remember that it was meant to be just a goodnight kiss. . .nothing else.

When they drew apart he said jerkily, 'I'll watch you safely inside and then I'll be off, my love.'

She nodded, and on legs that weren't quite steady she went down the path and put her key in the door, then she turned and waved and he saluted her back. As he strode off into the summer night Helen was left with her thoughts, and they'd never been more confusing.

He'd called her 'my love', she thought as she undressed. Had he meant it, or did Daniel scatter endearments around lightly? If the way he'd kissed her was anything to go by he'd meant it, or was she so bemused with the magic of *Hiawatha* that she was seeing romance in everything?

She awoke on Sunday morning with a delicious feeling of well-being and lay watching the sun dappling the ceiling as she recalled the happenings of the previous night. James had done her a favour, she supposed. If he hadn't gone storming off she wouldn't have met Daniel. . .and they wouldn't have watched *Hiawatha* together. . .he wouldn't have taken her home. . .kissed her goodnight. . .

Helen took her breakfast into the garden, and as she drank fresh orange juice and crunched brown toast she was thinking how much she owed to the quiet park behind her hedge. Her jog that morning and Thomas's fall into the lake had been their introduction, and last night she'd spent the happiest night in years there. Yes, she had a lot to thank Linnias Park for.

At half-past ten the phone rang, which was not entirely unexpected as she was on call. It was Mike Norton. 'Sorry to break into your Sunday, Helen,' he said, 'but a sickle cell anaemia has just come in and it's a pretty bad attack.'

Helen Blake the doctor quickly replaced the woman on cloud nine. 'I'll be right over, Mike,' she promised briskly. 'Is it one of the regulars?'

'Leroy Bennet ring a bell?'

'Yes, it does.'

'The kid's in a lot of severe back pain and is vomiting heavily.'

'Is Jill there?' Helen asked. 'She's been present when I've treated him before. Do her no harm to have a look this time.'

'Day off,' he said briefly. 'Probably sleeping the sleep of the triumphant if she won the bet.'

Helen smiled. Jill might be sleeping, but not triumphantly, at least with regards to Daniel. She was already fishing around for her car keys. 'Be with you in ten minutes,' she told him.

The seven-year-old West African boy had suffered several crises over a period of months and had always been in great pain with fever and vomiting when admitted to St Margaret's, and this time was no exception, though his general health was good between attacks.

'Prompt treatment in these cases is vital,' Helen told Mike as she examined the child. 'I'm going to start him on intravenous infusions to replace the fluids he's lost with the vomiting and diarrhoea, and antibiotics to prevent infection. There is a decrease in blood oxygenation so he'll need oxygen.

'On previous occasions the treatment I've just outlined has brought him through the crisis. Let's hope that it works this time, because the first time it doesn't it will mean an exchange blood transfusion to effect a short-term replacement of haemoglobin "S".'

Helen was inserting a cannula into a vein in Leroy's forearm and Mike said in a low voice, 'These inherited diseases are ghastly, aren't they?'

'Sure are,' she agreed as she bent over the patient. 'A child only gets sickle cell anaemia if both parents have it, or alternatively have the sickle cell trait. People of Leroy's race, and to a lesser degree the West Indian population, are advised to have a blood-test to see if they carry the gene before producing any offspring, but they don't always take notice, I'm afraid.'

The boy's dark face was glistening with perspiration, his body convulsed with pain, especially in the lower spine which she'd noticed was tender when she examined him.

'I'm giving him codeine and aspirin for the pain and hopefully it will soon subside.'

'It's the first time I've seen a case of this,' Mike said thoughtfully. 'I've read it up, of course. It's detected when a blood smear shows the red cells to be distorted into a sickle shape, isn't it?'

'Yes,' she agreed as he placed the oxygen mask over the boy's face. 'The red cells of those affected by the disease contain an abnormal type of haemoglobin, and if it crystallises in the blood capillaries where there is less oxygen the cells become distorted in a sickle shape which makes them frail and easily demolished.

'The sickle-shaped cells also have difficulty passing through the minute blood vessels, which causes blockage of the blood supply to various organs, creating a crisis such as our little one here is experiencing.'

She patted the boy's hand gently. 'But if this attack follows the same pattern as the others the pain and the fever will gradually subside, and he'll be able to go home in a few days. He'll have to keep up with the folic acid that he's already on. It's a lifetime thing, I'm afraid, that. He'll always be on it. And he'll continue to be a regular outpatient.

'So it's the recipe as before, Mike, and we'll see how he goes on.'

The young doctor looked pale and tired. 'How long since you slept?' she asked.

He smiled wearily. 'Can't say exactly. I'll have to consult my diary.'

She smiled back, but there was concern in it. 'Seriously, Mike?'

'Managed a few hours night before last.'

Helen frowned. Long shifts for junior doctors were nothing new. She'd gone through the same thing, still did sometimes, but everybody knew that a tired doctor wasn't an efficient one.

'Don't worry, Helen. I finish at two o'clock, at which time I shall return to my celibate cell to recharge my batteries,' he said wryly, but with a visible brightening at the thought.

'Good. See that you do,' she said crisply. On the point of departing, Helen turned in the doorway. 'By the way, if Jill tries to tell you that she won the wager. . .she didn't.'

Mike was perking up by the minute. 'Our Jilly didn't crack it with Danny Boy? How do you know?'

'I was there,' she told him briefly, and before he had time to hold a post-mortem on that titbit of information she went.

By the time she got back to the cottage the park was filling up with folks out to enjoy a warm Sunday and she began to feel restless. Perhaps if she walked across the park she might see Daniel and the children, she thought, or another way of seeing him might be to call and see how Bruno was, but she knew she wasn't going to do either. She was going to stay put and do some chores, and the first one was going to be some gardening. In denim dungarees, old shoes and her floppy straw hat, she sallied forth, but it was hot work, and after an hour of hoeing and weeding Helen sank down on to a chair to cool off.

'You look as if a long cool drink is required,' Daniel's voice said from the gate and her heart leapt with pleasure. She hadn't had to go to him. He'd come to find her.

She knew that she looked hot and crumpled, but her voice was calm as she called back, 'Yes, it is. I'm just trying to work up the energy to go inside for one.'

He was coming along the path towards her with his casual stride, and as she looked at the fair bronzed bulk of him Helen thought he would make heads turn wherever he went, and the odds were he wouldn't even be aware of it. Daniel was an uncomplicated man, and there weren't many of them about. She felt ashamed when she thought back to how he'd irritated her when they'd first met. She'd jumped to all sorts of wrong conclusions, and it would have served her right if he'd had nothing to do with her.

He was in shorts and a T-shirt again, and when he planted himself in front of her Helen saw that his legs were straight and strong, his waist flat, his chest broad . . .a big man with a big heart. Would there be room in it for her? she wondered.

'Well, what is it to be?' he said as she slumped there looking up at him. 'Shall I go inside and get you one, or shall we go to the pub?'

Helen uncoiled herself, straightened her hat, and hitched up her braces. 'I can't go to the pub. I'm on call.'

'Got your bleeper, haven't you?'

'Er. . .yes.'

'Well, come on, then.'

'I need to shower.'

'Sure. Carry on. I can wait. Need any help?' he asked with a grin.

Helen had the insane urge to say, Yes, I'd like us to bathe together. . .sleep together. . .be together. . . always, but the answer came out as a cool, 'No, thanks, I can manage.'

He gave his deep chuckle. 'I come highly recommended. The boys think I'm the best back-scrubber in —'

'No,' she interrupted him. 'Stay put, I won't be long,' and wondered what would have happened if she'd taken him up on the offer. Her body went warm at the thought.

'OK, then,' he agreed amiably. 'Chop chop.' And, lifting the straw hat off her head, he placed it upon his own golden locks and settled himself into her vacant chair.

'Where are the children?' she called over her shoulder as she went towards the house.

'Gone to a party. I have to pick them up at half-past four. We'll soon be doing the honours ourselves. Jonathan has a birthday coming up in the not too distant future.'

'Really? How old will he be?'

'Six, and he's counting the days.'

When Helen went back downstairs, refreshed from the shower, dungarees and old shoes discarded for a pink sundress and black open sandals, she saw that Daniel was asleep, head thrown back, chest moving rhythmically up and down, and the hat over his face.

Her mouth softened. There couldn't be much time for relaxation in his life. It would do him good to have a nap, and so she seated herself near by with a book.

An hour had gone by and she was still on the same page, too aware of Daniel to concentrate on anything else. Her eyes were on the hands resting loosely on his knees, surgeon's hands, strong and skilful, as were her own to a lesser degree.

Maybe the bond between them wasn't frail at all. They were both in the same profession. She was already captivated by his children, and as for the man himself. . . he'd certainly brought *her* out of her dry chrysalis. She hadn't felt so alive in years, but the question was. . . did she have the same effect on Daniel?

Suddenly he was awake, watching her from beneath the brim of the hat, blue eyes rueful. He yawned. 'How long have I been asleep?'

'An hour.'

He pulled himself up right. 'Oh, hell!'

'It's all right,' she assured him with a smile. '*I* don't mind.'

'Yes, but *I* do. I was supposed to be taking you to the pub.'

'I'll make us a snack here, if you like,' Helen offered.

He smiled back sleepily. 'I like.'

Daniel followed her into the house and as she bustled around the kitchen Helen was conscious of him in her small sitting-room studying Adam's photograph again.

'What about this guy, Helen?' he asked.

'What about him?' she parried.

'The one and only, was he?'

'I cared deeply for him, yes. I imagine that's how you were with Marianne?'

He sighed. 'Yes, but you weren't the only one who had competition.'

Helen stared at him. 'You mean another man?'

'No. I'm talking about a racket striking a ball over a wide green net.'

'Tennis?'

'Yes. She had all the time in the world for Thomas and Jonathan, but I felt sometimes that I was just fitted in between matches. I might have imagined it, I suppose.'

There was silence as Helen digested that statement, and then she said slowly, 'If that *was* the case she was very foolish.'

Daniel raised a surprised eyebrow. 'Why foolish? You might have felt the same. Being a doctor's wife isn't always a bed of roses, is it?'

'No, I don't suppose it is,' she told him quietly, heart thudding at the implication of his words. There was only one thing that would ever have made him come second if *she'd* been his wife. It was something he would understand, and recklessly she told him.

'The sick might have come before you, Daniel,' she told him as colour washed up in her face, 'as their needs are always greater than ours, but I would have been there for you in every other part of life.'

This was dangerous ground and Daniel had led her on to it. Had she given herself away? She was placing spoonfuls of fluffy scrambled eggs on to toast and he came up behind her and brushed the back of her neck with his lips. 'Yes, I do believe you would,' he said softly, 'but we both know the pressures of the job, don't we? And as for the present it's a shame that our lives aren't a bit less cluttered.'

Helen swung round. 'Cluttered?'

'Well, yes. You still carrying the torch for Kerwin. . . and I have my two small appendages, but — ' he pointed to the food ' — it's going cold. Shall we eat?'

She nodded numbly. It appeared that it wasn't the moment to start expostulating that she wasn't in love with a dead man. . .and that his 'appendages' were delightful. It would look too much as if she was pleading her case, and she had too much pride to do that, so the meal progressed in silence.

Each time Helen looked up Daniel's eyes were on her and there was puzzlement in their blue depths, but he didn't put his confusion into words and she wasn't going to help him out.

At last he said with a quizzical smile, 'Looks as if we're in for an early winter. The temperature seems to be dropping.'

'I hadn't noticed,' she told him, straight-faced.

'That's because you're not sitting where I am.'

Helen found herself laughing. It was impossible to be distant with him for long, and in any case she didn't want to be distant, she wanted to be close to him, near him always, part of his. . . Stop it! she told herself. For all you know it's completely one-sided. Daniel might have made one or two meaningful remarks but the rapport could be all in your imagination.

He was glancing at his watch. 'Must go, Helen, fatherhood calls. My two rascals will be spilling forth with their party-bags in a short space of time, and then for the rest of the day it will be my turn for chores as Bruno's incapacitated.' His voice deepened. 'I've enjoyed this short time in your quiet oasis, and am loath to depart, but no doubt we'll meet in Disneyland tomorrow, eh?'

She gave him her wide, brilliant smile. 'Yes, I'd say there's nothing surer than that. . . St Margaret's calling.'

Helen walked to the gate with him and as they stood beneath the arch of wild roses that spanned it she was acutely conscious that Daniel had kissed her on that very spot the night before.

If he did remember he didn't show it. He was reaching into the pocket of his shorts and out came a small leather-bound book with gilt-edged pages. He took hold of Helen's hand and placed it solemnly on her palm. 'Longfellow's poems,' he said by way of explanation. 'I knew I had it somewhere, and after a bit of rummaging around this morning I found it.'

Her eyes were alight with pleasure. 'For me?'

'Who else but? I bought it when I was a student, and now, having found someone who loves Longfellow as much as myself, I thought I'd pass it on.'

'That's lovely, Daniel, thank you,' she said softly.

Last night his departing gesture had been a kiss, today a book of poems. He really was the most unpredictable man. Their glances held, his steady and unwavering, hers bright and uncertain, and she wondered if he was going to kiss her again, but he didn't; with a brief wave he started to walk away.

He moved easily among the pleasuring crowds, his corn-coloured hair and broad shoulders standing out among them, and as Helen curled her fingers around the small book her smile was tender.

CHAPTER EIGHT

THE week that followed was a busy one. A small epidemic of meningococcal meningitis meant Pluto Ward being cleared to cope with the influx, and caused Joanne, the young anorexic, to complain that it would be worth eating her food just to get out of the overcrowded Pinocchio Ward.

'Well, see that you do,' Helen had told her. 'Your Grandma has been contacted and she'd love to have you with her, but you've got to get your weight back first.'

The first meningitis patient, a young boy called Luke, had been admitted with a stiff neck, fever, and a blotchy scarlet rash on his body. The cerebrospinal fluid taken from his spinal cord in a lumbar puncture had shown which strain of bacterial meningitis was present and Helen had ordered a huge dosage of intravenous penicillin.

No sooner had he been diagnosed and treatment commenced than three other cases were admitted, and staff advised that others could follow.

Helen saw little of Daniel in the first part of the week as both had full theatre lists and new admissions were coming in all the time, but whenever they did bump into each other the meetings, though short, were sweet, with the new rapport between them bringing tranquillity instead of tension to their working lives.

On Thursday morning he sent for her, and when she received the summons her heart lifted. She was feeling tired and frustrated at the lack of time they were spending together, and when he greeted her with the question, 'How would you like to be in on a Fallot's tetralogy?' her face lit up.

'Yes, of course,' she said immediately.

Not only would it be valuable experience, but the pleasure of working with him would be indescribable. His clear blue gaze was taking in her pallor and the shadows beneath the huge hazel eyes and he questioned, 'It's been a busy week. Are you all right, Helen?'

I am now, she wanted to say, but instead she said, 'Tell me about it, Daniel?' and when he continued to study her without speaking she prompted, 'The Fallot's tetralogy.'

He brought his mind back from wherever it had been wandering with an effort. 'Oh, yes, the heart patient. The echocardiogram has shown the usual four defects, and the organ is the usual boot shape that one finds with this sort of case, also there is cyanosis and clubbing of the fingers and toes. The youngster is being admitted on Monday on the strength of the tests, and I'd like you to assist during the surgery. You're not on call this weekend, are you?' he asked.

She felt herself go warm. Daniel was going to ask her out. 'No, why?'

'No reason. Just see that you get some rest, that's all.'

Disappointment filled her, and it didn't disappear when he said, 'We're off to visit an elderly aunt of mine who has requested to see her great-nephews, so the Reed family, plus a slightly improved Bruno, are off for a very low-key weekend at Bexhill-on-Sea.'

'Oh, I see,' Helen said flatly as she told herself that a visit from Daniel last Sunday didn't mean it was going to be a regular occurrence.

On Saturday night she went to the cinema with Janice and the girls, shared Sunday lunch with her parents, and in the evening took a solitary stroll through the park.

Tall, slender as a flower shoot, in the palest of green suits that brought out the glints in her soft dark bob, Helen walked by the lake. She could see the chimneys of Daniel's house across its still water, and it was inevitable that her feet led her in that direction.

There was no sign of life as she passed the back gates, but when she came to the drive on the side, curving to the front door, she took a step backwards. The car was on the drive and Daniel was unloading the boot, while Bruno, obviously still in some discomfort, was easing himself out of the front passenger seat.

Helen went hot with embarrassment. They must have only just got back and here she was hovering at the gate. It called for a quick retreat, but she wasn't fast enough. Bruno had seen her.

'Hi, Helen!' he called as he pulled himself to his feet, and at the greeting Daniel swung round from the boot.

He looked tired and irritable, but managed a frayed smile. 'Thank God for a vision of cool sanity,' he breathed. She would have preferred to be a vision of beauty or charm, but, if 'cool sanity' was the prescription he needed, she could be that.

'What's wrong?' she asked as she approached.

Bruno laughed. 'It was not the good idea to go to Bexhill, eh, Daniel?' and, throwing one of his devastating smiles in her direction, he picked up a hold-all and limped off into the house.

'Is that so?' she enquired.

Daniel raised his head out of the boot. 'That's putting it mildly. I'm suffering from an overdose of Aunt Evelyn's parrot, Pekinese, and her penchant for telling

me at regular intervals that I ought to replace the boys'
beloved Bruno with a "motherly body", and while I'm
at it find myself a good woman to replace the mother of
my unruly children.'

Helen's heart was racing but she answered him
casually enough. 'A motherly body *and* a good woman
sound like a bit too much of a worthy thing.' Her voice
rose. 'And Thomas and Jonathan *aren't* unruly — and by
the way, where are they?'

He nodded towards the back seat of the car. 'In
there. . .blotto. We went to the beach to let off steam
before we set off back and they've tired themselves out.'

Walking round to the side, he lifted the sleeping
Jonathan carefully into his arms and said, 'They're a bit
grubby, but I think straight to bed, don't you?'

'Yes. It would be a shame to disturb them,' Helen
agreed, and as he strode off towards the house it seemed
the most natural thing in the world to pick up the small
Thomas and follow him.

Daniel glanced over his shoulder as he went up the
front steps and his eyes warmed when he saw Thomas in
her arms. 'Thanks, Helen,' he said tiredly, 'you're
heaven-sent. Bruno's not a lot of use at the moment,
though it's not his fault.

'I suppose it's possible that my aunt thought a "motherly body's" muscles might be less susceptible than
those of a young Adonis, and that "good women" who
would be prepared to take on the work and responsi-
bility of a ready-made family grow on trees.'

By now they were placing the sleeping children in
their beds and Helen's face was in shadow as she bent
over Thomas. 'A woman who really loved you would
love your children too,' she said quietly.

'That is how I would want it,' he said sombrely. 'Not a

strong maternal love that was prepared for me to tag along.'

Was that supposed to be a warning, she wondered, or was he talking about Marianne? She'd already told him that if he'd been in *her* life he would have come first.

Hadn't he noticed that she was no longer critical of him, she thought as they went downstairs together; that she admired and respected him. . .loved him, or was he too blinkered with the past and the responsibilities of the present?

One thing was for sure: he was going to have to see it for himself. Her experience with Adam had made her wary of relationships without commitment. She couldn't bear the thought of being adrift on that sort of sea again.

'You look very swish, Helen,' Bruno said when she went into the kitchen. It took her mind back to their evening in the steak house and her spirits lifted. That was more like it. The 'cool, sane' mantle didn't fit so well tonight.

She was hot with longing for the nicest man she'd ever known, and after the conversation they'd just had 'insane' seemed a more fitting word to describe her, for expecting anything to come of it.

Bruno had put steaks under the grill and was preparing a salad, when Daniel's voice said from behind, 'Stay and eat with us, Helen. We're sick of our own company.'

'Yes, if you want me to,' she said lightly, not sure that she wanted to be an antidote for boredom, but deciding if she couldn't have the cake the crumbs would do.

Daniel's good humour surfaced again during the meal and as they ate the food and shared a bottle of wine Helen found herself relaxing in the company of the two men. Bruno did most of the talking, telling them about life in Germany as part of a large family, and as she and Daniel listened Helen was conscious of his warm blue gaze on her.

'I must go,' she said when the meal was over and they'd cleared away. She knew that Daniel was tired, and the odds were they had another stressful week ahead at St Margaret's. The meningitis outbreak had been very worrying. Some of the small patients were still giving cause for concern and were being carefully monitored.

'I'll walk you home,' Daniel said.

'No,' she protested. 'On Friday you told me to get some rest; now I'm telling you to do the same, and I'd take some milk and biscuits up with you in case the boys are hungry in the middle of the night, having missed their meal.'

He touched his forelock meekly. 'Yes, Doctor. Any other instructions?' and she was reminded of the homily she'd given him about antibiotics that first day when Thomas had fallen into the lake.

She laughed. 'No, that's all for now, and I *must* be going.'

'You didn't refuse to let me take you home after *Hiawatha*,' he protested.

She faced him with a clear, grave gaze. 'I was on cloud nine that night. . .the music, the words, the warm park. . .'

'And tonight you're not?'

'It seems to be a state of affairs that doesn't last.'

He was smiling his quirky smile. 'We'll have to see if something can't be done about that, then, and by the way. . .'

'Yes?'

'I heard Bruno telling you that you looked "swish".'

She didn't answer, and he continued, 'I'd say it was a feat of understatement,' and he traced his finger gently along her cheek.

Helen felt tears clutch at her throat. Their relationship seemed to be a sequence of two steps forward and one step back, and in that moment she vowed that if *she* had any choice in the matter it would move in only one direction. . .forward.

'Ring me when you get in,' he called as she went through the gates.

'Daniel! It's broad daylight, and the park is full of people.'

'Nevertheless. Three rings, and I'll know you're back safely.'

'And what if I don't ring?' she teased.

He grinned back. 'I shall demonstrate how it's possible to run on water.'

In the days that followed they *didn't* take any backward steps. Helen and Daniel worked together, and occasionally socialised along with his children, in a harmony that helped to banish her earlier frustrations.

At his suggestion, whenever possible they lunched together, and if time allowed strolled through the hospital grounds for a breath of air before returning to their patients.

The summer days came and went, warm and dry with the occasional dazzling shower, and sometimes in the evenings Daniel and the boys cycled across the park to her cottage where they played happily in the garden under the watchful eye of Forceps the cat.

As she played with the children Helen often looked up to find him deep in thought, and they were always thoughts that he didn't seem to want to share. He always kissed her as they were leaving, a gentle, passionless sort of kiss, which warned her to quench the fires that his touch kindled within her.

Helen wanted more than that from him, but she knew she could wait until he'd broken down the barriers that were keeping them as friends rather than lovers.

Their increasing closeness had been noted by those she encountered on the wards and in the staffroom and she good-naturedly accepted teasing from Mike and John. 'I'll have to get my suit out of pawn if Danny Boy wants me to be best man,' Mike had said one day, and John in his dry way had asked if they'd like matching scalpels as a wedding present.

Jill Morrison had listened to their banter with a set face and made no comment, and Helen had become aware that the pert young blonde hadn't given up on Daniel. She'd kept a low profile after losing her wager with Mike and John regarding the park theatre, but it was possible that she only saw it as a temporary set-back.

It was Friday morning, and when Helen went into Pinocchio Ward at eight o'clock the night sister who was waiting to go off duty beckoned her into the office.

The bed that had been Joanne's was empty. She had regained enough of her weight loss to be discharged, and with the permission of social workers and an indifferent agreement from her parents had been placed in the care of her grandmother who had come all the way from Newcastle-upon-Tyne to fetch her. She had been a much happier child when she left and Helen was hoping that the new arrangement might be the end of her troubles.

Helen touched the coverlet gently as she passed. 'Good luck, Joanne,' she breathed.

The sister informed her that Daniel had already been in to check on a patient that he'd operated on the previous day, and Helen looked at her in surprise. Today was his private patients' clinic at his rooms in the town centre, but obviously he'd had to satisfy himself first that all was well with the child in question.

'He left a note for you,' she said, 'as he knew this would be your first stop.'

Helen felt her cheeks reddening. 'Instructions about one of the patients, I suppose,' she said casually.

There was a curious gleam in the other woman's eye. She wasn't having that. 'What, in a sealed envelope?'

'Er. . .yes. . .well. . . I'll. . .' And Helen took the envelope out of Sister's hand and walked off.

There was a note inside the envelope.

Will you come to Jonathan's birthday party on Sunday? Protective clothing and shin-pads recommended. Sorry to be so late with the invitation. I've been intending mentioning it for days. Unfortunately Bruno won't be on hand. A student friend of his is over from Germany and I've foolishly given him the weekend off. By the way, the birthday boy has specially requested your presence.
Daniel

Helen smiled. She would love to go to Jonathan's party, and at the first opportunity would ask how she could assist.

'You can assist best by just being there, Helen,' Daniel told her when she rang to accept. 'Jonathan has invited six of the boys from the school he attends. We haven't been living in the area long enough for him to have too many friends.' His voice deepened. 'It will be my first venture into this kind of thing since we became a one-parent family. Marianne was there for them last year.'

He'd said it quite matter-of-factly but she could imagine the expression on his face. It was the sort of look she'd often seen on her own countenance, but Daniel had helped her to lay *her* ghost. Would she be able to do the same for him?

'And you've got it all organised?' she asked.

'Sure,' he said breezily. 'I've done a marathon shop, and have got some interesting games lined up, so I'm not anticipating any hiccups.'

'Fine, I'll see you there, then.'

She decided against a padded vest and shin-pads, choosing instead a Paisley blouse in soft pastel shades, and a long moss-green skirt that swirled around her as she walked. Gold hoops in her ears and gold strappy sandals on her feet completed the ensemble.

When she inspected herself before departure Helen saw an attractive woman in the mirror, dark hair gleaming, eyes glowing, her long slenderness shown off to advantage in the clothes she was wearing, and as she picked up her bag and let herself out of the cottage the afternoon ahead seemed like the most exciting thing she'd ever attended.

Walking around the lake to get to Daniel's house, Helen saw that the park was filling up with old folk, young folk, and families out to enjoy a warm Sunday afternoon.

As she passed the spot where Thomas had fallen in the lake she eyed the still green water fondly. Hadn't its magnetism for a small boy brought Daniel and herself together?

She'd bought Jonathan a remote-controlled car, and a smaller model of it for Thomas. Watching a younger child trying to understand why *they* weren't receiving gifts on a brother or sister's birthday wasn't a thing she liked to see.

Helen let herself in at the same back gate that she'd entered with Bruno on that fateful first day and saw that outdoor games had been arranged on the lawn, and at the top end of the garden on the patio beside the house a long table had been set up with a gaily coloured cloth on it.

Yes, he *was* organised, she thought. Beneath that easygoing exterior was someone just as orderly as herself, and it was a comforting thought.

The assumption lasted exactly two minutes. The kitchen door was wide open and Helen thought she might as well go in that way as any other. As she stepped inside her jaw dropped. The room was a shambles. There wasn't an inch of clear space on the units. The kitchen table was groaning under the weight of food waiting to be prepared, and in the midst of it, looking decidedly harassed, was 'mine host'.

'Oh, dear! What a mess!' she exclaimed.

Daniel swung round at the sound of her voice and she saw that he was holding a fork with a charred-looking sausage on the end of it.

'Helen!' he uttered. '*Am* I glad to see you!'

'Yes, I can imagine,' she said drily, her plans for a pleasant afternoon disappearing like water down the plughole. 'Am I to take it that there's been a hiccup?'

'Right in one,' he said glumly. 'The whole morning has been a catastrophe. I went to the shops for one or two last-minute things and the car broke down. I had to have it towed to a garage and get a taxi back. The boys are over-excited and have been playing me up, and then to cap it all——' he gazed forlornly at the blackened sausage '—one of the guest's mothers rang up to check on the time of the party and I let the sausages burn.'

Helen was reaching for a huge butcher's apron hanging behind the door. She didn't know whether to laugh or feel sorry for him. *He* hadn't laughed or even smiled once since she'd arrived. His marvellous good humour was in short supply.

'Where are the boys?' she asked as she started dealing with the food.

'Playing, up in the bedroom.'

'Are they dressed?'

'No, not yet.'

'We've got thirty minutes to get this show on the road, Daniel,' she said crisply, 'so if you supervise their dressing I'll carry on here, and let's hope that none of the guests is early.'

'I'll second that,' he said fervently, and, dropping a swift kiss on her cheek, he made for the door. It was one occasion when the swift caress didn't have the usual impact. She'd just been to the fridge and discovered that the door wasn't shut properly and the jellies were all swimmy.

It was hot work dashing in and out laying the food on the table outside once she'd prepared it, but there was no time to stop. Any moment the guests would be arriving, and once eight small boys were together there would be no time for anything. Her hair was beginning to feel damp and sticky, and the cool Paisley blouse felt hot and restricting.

Helen was standing red-cheeked in front of the grill

doing a fresh lot of sausages when a voice that was anything but welcome to her ears drawled, 'I see you're making yourself useful.'

Jill Morrison looked cool, confident, and very smart in a white sheath dress with huge gold buttons, and when Helen saw her standing there anger ripped through her. 'Yes, I am,' she said steelily. 'If I weren't there wouldn't be any party, as it was chaos when I arrived.'

'Good for you,' Jill said with a patronising air that made Helen want to slap her. 'Carry on the good work. I'll see you later. I'm just going to give Daniel and the kids moral support when the guests arrive.'

'I wasn't aware that you'd been invited,' Helen said, squirming as a splash of hot fat landed on her nose.

'You mean to say Daniel didn't tell you?' she asked with bland innocence. 'I suppose he thought the boys might feel the absence of their mother and that a sympathetic woman's presence would be welcome.'

Helen didn't believe that. Daniel might have invited her for some reason, but never as a mother-substitute. It made her shudder to think of Jill having any part in the lives of the two little boys. Sympathetic was the last word she would use to describe her.

But no way was she going to let her see that she was getting under her skin, and so she said casually, 'Really? Is that so?' while at the same time inspecting a trivet of golden-brown sausages that she'd just removed from under the grill. 'If that's the case then don't let me keep you,' she told Jill. 'Daniel is getting the children ready. They should be down any moment.'

As her tormentor strolled off Helen thought that the day's promise was already wearing thin. She was beginning to feel miserable. Helping out was no problem, but

Daniel just leaving her to it, and Jill Morrison's unwelcome appearance, which she would have thought Daniel would have at least mentioned, were bringing her down to earth with a bump.

The only thing left to do were the sandwiches. Everything else was done, and as her fingers flew Thomas and Jonathan appeared in the doorway. They looked fresh and bonny in white cotton shirts and grey shorts and as they smiled up at her it was all she could do to stop herself from hugging them.

'Are you the hostess with the mostest, Helen?' Jonathan asked. 'Daddy says you are.'

Her smile flashed out. 'It doesn't look like it, does it? I'd say head cook and bottle-washer describes me more exactly.' She wiped her hands on the big striped apron. 'I've got something for you both. The biggest one is for you, Jonathan, as you're the birthday boy, and the other is for Thomas.'

'Can we open them?' they wanted to know.

'I would imagine so, but check with Dad first, eh?'

Dad had changed too, and when he appeared almost on their heels Helen felt as if she was the only one who looked a mess. Daniel was wearing a blue short-sleeved shirt that matched his eyes, and khaki shorts. He looked cool, trim, and disturbingly attractive, a far cry from the harassed chef who had greeted her a short time ago, and a much more casual figure than Jill in the white dress.

'What have they got to ask me?' he asked with a smile of relief as he saw that order had prevailed.

'If they can open their presents.'

'Yes, of course, and if the shapes of the parcels are anything to go by I can tell that you know what small boys like.' He was looking around the kitchen. 'You're a gem for taking charge the way you did, Helen. I can't believe we're actually ready on time.'

She was taking ice-cream out of the freezer and said the first thing that came into her mind. 'You didn't tell me that Jill was coming to the party.'

'The reason for that is. . .' he began, but didn't get the chance to finish. The doorbell was ringing. The first guests had arrived.

Helen saw little of the party. Every time she was about to emerge from the kitchen more juice was needed or more sandwiches. Then she was hunting around for matches to light the candles on the birthday cake, and once the candles had been blown out it was time to cut it up for distribution on departure.

She spoke with Daniel twice during the proceedings — once when he came dashing into the kitchen for a ball of string for one of the games, and said briefly, 'Where do they get their energy from, Helen? I'm flagging already. I'm beginning to think we should have invited some of the mothers to stay.'

She smiled. 'Most mothers are only too pleased to deposit their offspring for a couple of hours without getting embroiled.'

He wiped a damp brow. 'I suppose you can't blame 'em for that. My hair stands on end when I think of how I'd have coped without you.'

'Let Jill take charge of the games for a while,' she suggested.

'What? In those heels?' he hooted, and was gone.

His second appearance had more important connotations. With the children milling around him noisily Daniel called from the doorway, 'I can't see Thomas anywhere. He must have wandered off. Will you find him for me, Helen?'

Her heart skipped a beat. Wandered off? He wouldn't have gone out of the garden surely? She would check the house first before allowing herself to become alarmed.

As she whizzed past the door that led to the garden Helen saw Jill peering lethargically among the bushes. You'll have to do better than that, madam, she thought angrily, if you're bent on being a 'mother figure'.

The ground floor of the house yielded no sign of the missing Thomas, but as Helen flew up the stairs she smiled with relief. A small figure was fast asleep on the landing, golden head resting in the crook of his arm.

She picked him up carefully, and as she cradled him in her arms he snuggled closer and gave a contented sigh. Daniel was waiting for them at the bottom as she carried him downstairs, his own relief mirrored in his face, but as they drew level Helen saw an expression in his eyes that might have been envy though she couldn't think why.

'You love my kids, don't you, Helen?' he said with a sort of bleak gravity, and without giving her time to reply he took Thomas off her and placed him on the sofa in the lounge.

Yes, I do, she wanted to say, because they're young, vulnerable, and quite delightful, but most of all I love them because I love their father.

It wasn't the right moment, though, and she thought ruefully that it never was. Feet were flying in from the garden. It was time to sort out the bags of little surprises and get the children's coats. The party was over, and as Helen gave the last child his things her spirits plummeted as she saw Jill queening it beside Daniel as he said his goodbyes.

Some hostess with the mostest I've turned out to be,

she thought wryly as she wiped the worktops down. The cleaner who's getting meaner suits me better, but at least I've earned my crust today, which is more than little Jilly can say, though I haven't found time to eat it!

When Helen went into the hall Jill was smiling provocatively up at Daniel, her buoyancy restored now that the party was over, but Helen couldn't see his expression as his back was towards her, though from the set of the broad shoulders he looked relaxed and happy enough. The third member of the tableau was watching them with wide eyes that were staring straight ahead in a small, set face, and as if aware of his scrutiny Jill swung round and took his hand.

'Shall we go to see if Thomas is awake, Jonathan?' she cooed.

'He's not,' he told her with a scowl, and, disengaging his hand from hers, he marched upstairs.

Jill's face flushed and sudden anger glinted in her eyes, but her voice was full of sweet reasonableness as she said, 'I suppose he's tired too. Shall I put him to bed?'

Daniel guffawed. 'Good gracious, no! He won't thank you for that at only five o'clock on his birthday. He's just a bit over-excited, that's all. A quiet half-hour with his presents and he'll be fine, and, as for the rest of us, I think a drink is called for, don't you, Helen?'

So he *was* aware of her presence, she thought. He knew she had surfaced at last. She shook her head. 'No, thanks, Daniel. I'll be off. I want to freshen up.' Helen's feelings were in a jumble. She felt frazzled, yet deflated because the party was over, confused about the strange look Daniel had given her as she'd carried Thomas downstairs. . .and ashamed that pushy Jill Morrison was making her lose her cool. She wasn't prepared to watch her ogling Daniel and trying to win the children over. On another occasion she might have the stamina for it, but not today.

'Do change your mind,' he coaxed. 'I'll go and get some glasses and we'll drink to a very successful venture.'

As he disappeared in the direction of the dining-room with Jill at his heels like a yappy white poodle, Helen let herself out of the house and walked slowly down the drive.

The sun had gone in. The sky was overcast with leaden clouds for the first time in weeks and she thought ruefully that she and the weather were in tune.

Daniel rang at half-past seven as she was listlessly wondering what to do with the evening, and when she heard his voice her bones melted with longing. Whatever made him tick, she loved this man, but if she was going to retain her sanity she had better calm down. . . no more wearing her heart on her sleeve.

'You rushed off and left us, Helen,' he said. 'Why? The boys were disappointed to find you gone. I'd hoped we could all spend the rest of the evening together.'

She swallowed. She wanted to tell him that she would have liked that more than he would ever know, but, because she was still smarting a little, her defence mechanisms took over and she said flippantly, 'By *all* I take it you mean yourself, myself, the children, and. . . the mother figure?'

There was silence at the other end of the line and then he said slowly, 'What "mother figure"?'

Helen was on a crash course to disaster and couldn't stop herself. 'You mean to say you don't know? Why, Jill, of course.'

'I see,' he said heavily. 'I was about to explain her

presence when we were interrupted, if you remember. She *wasn't* invited. Jill gatecrashed the party. She heard me discussing it with your friend Janice the other day. Since she's had youngsters of her own, I was asking her advice, and Janice asked me jokingly if anyone could come, and, joking back, I said "the more the merrier", and Jill being Jill, she took me up on it.

'I rang to thank you for taking charge when I'd made such a hash of things. I couldn't come over as the boys are in bed and Bruno isn't back yet. It seemed like old times, a lovely woman bustling around the kitchen, but I seem to have taken too much for granted. I'm sorry.'

As she'd listened to his explanation Helen had felt black misery washing over her. She'd been petty and ungracious and couldn't wait to apologise, but he was bidding her a brief goodbye, and then there was silence.

CHAPTER NINE

AFTER a sleepless night Helen was up much earlier than usual, and with time to spare before setting off for St Margaret's she went into the garden and through the gate into the park. The red roofs of Daniel's house were visible among the trees at the other side of the lake, and she thought that if Bruno still wasn't back the man she loved would be busy giving his children breakfast and starting them on their day.

Had *he* slept? she wondered. Probably, because he'd nothing to reproach himself for, had he? If he *had* been responsible for inviting Jill, he was still entitled to ask whoever he liked to his son's birthday party.

It was just gone half-past seven and the phone ringing brought her dashing back inside, heart thumping as she prayed that it might be him, but it was her mother, sounding tense and uneasy.

'Have you watched the news on TV this morning, Helen?' she asked.

She frowned. 'No, I've been in the garden. Why?'

'That's all right, then.'

'What do you mean, Mum? It's too early in the day for riddles. You ask if I've seen the early morning news, and then tell me it's of no matter.'

'I'm coming over; in fact we both are,' her mother said quickly. 'Wait for us,' and she put the phone down.

Helen sighed. What was all that about? She'd sounded most peculiar. Perhaps the health service was being disbanded and she was going to get the sack, or they'd found a new wonder drug that would make the population a hundred per cent healthy?

With the sight of her parents' set faces came the first stirrings of unease. Her father was going to be late for the surgery, she thought illogically. Surely her mother could have explained over the phone. She was desperate to see Daniel. Today of all days she didn't want to be late.

'Sit down, Helen,' her father said heavily. 'We have some disturbing news.'

The very tone of his voice struck dread in her. 'What is it?' she asked slowly.

'The newscaster said this morning that the snows have shifted on K2 and a body has been sighted. It's in the area where Adam was lost, and his name was mentioned.'

Helen went cold. Cold as the ice that had been his tomb for so long. Only a short time ago Daniel had helped her to lay Adam's ghost and she'd felt free of pain at last, but the past wasn't done with, was it? A great shudder went through her. Adam had no family. If there was need of an identification she might be asked to do it, and that was a horror she could do without.

Her parents were watching her, their faces full of distress, and her mother said gently, 'We know what you're thinking. That you want to remember Adam as you last saw him. . .young. . .vital. . .alive.'

She spoke for the first time. 'Yes, that *is* what I'm thinking. I've mourned him for so long, and just when I've fought free of him he's. . .' Her voice faltered.

'We don't know yet that it *is* Adam,' her father said. 'Try not to distress yourself, Helen. I'll make some enquiries and let you know.' His eyes went over her ashen face. 'Do you think you'd be better giving St Margaret's a miss today?'

Helen brought her mind back from a faraway land to the ordinary trappings of her life with an effort. 'No. No, of course not. I can't stay away from St Margaret's because of this. I'm needed there. . .and there's someone I *must* see.'

Margaret's shrewd eyes were on her daughter. 'After all this time you're in love again, aren't you, Helen?' she said.

'Yes, I am,' she told her with the candour that had always been between them, 'and I feel that it's horrendous if Adam's body should be found at this particular time, just when I'm. . .' She paused as a vision of hurt blue eyes came into her mind and then finished off, 'Trying to cope with it.'

In spite of the gravity of the moment her father smiled. 'What's this, then? Our daughter in love? Who's the lucky man?'

Not so lucky if her behaviour last night was anything to go by, Helen thought ruefully.

'Shall I make a guess?' her mother suggested.

'If you must.'

'A certain charming consultant? Daniel Reed?'

'Ten out of ten, Mum.'

'And you're not bothered that he already has a family?'

'No. Though the question doesn't arise at this moment in time. Our relationship is still in its very early stages, so please don't set too much store on it, will you?' Her glance went to the grandfather clock in the corner of the sitting-room and she got to her feet. 'And if I don't get moving I shall be late for my ward rounds.'

When her parents had gone Helen's veneer of calm

cracked. She'd always known that Adam's body still lay somewhere on the mountain, and in a strange sort of way she'd been glad that K2 was his last resting place because of his love of the icy peaks. But now, just as she was getting her life together again, nature might have another nasty trick up her sleeve.

All the way to St Margaret's she felt strange and disorientated, as if there were whiteness all around her, and *she* was being sucked down into it. She parked the car mechanically and made her way to the staffroom, aware that she was late, and far from being at her best.

There was an even more urgent need in her to see Daniel now. She'd been anxious to make things right between them after last night, but now she needed the calm, good-natured, strength of him to put the nightmare that had begun her day into perspective.

She was relieved to find the room empty. No way was she in the mood for idle chatter or provocative remarks from Jill. She'd had an overdose of that young woman over the weekend.

The feeling of blankness was still persisting and common sense told her it was shock. A cup of tea might be a good idea before she presented herself on the wards, and, acting on the thought, Helen went to the dispenser in the corridor. She sat down and drank it slowly. Already late, a few more minutes wouldn't make any difference.

The tea helped to steady her nerves but the feeling of unreality hadn't gone, and she thought that her father had been right. She should have stayed at home where she could have tuned into the news bulletins.

Helen started to shudder again. She really didn't want to hear the news. She wanted to blot it out. . .to pretend that her parents hadn't been round with the disturbing tidings, and there were two reasons for the way she felt.

First of all she'd laid Adam's ghost to rest, and put him out of her life for good, and having done that with Daniel's help she wanted it to stay that way. . .not have the mountain give up its dead.

The second reason was, as she'd told her parents, she was in love again, with a very special man; but a ready-made family, Jim Deardon smouldering in the back-ground, a predatory young house-officer stalking the man she loved, and the difference in personalities between Daniel and herself were enough complications to be going on with, without the discovery of Adam's body.

If it should turn out to be him she thought raggedly, it would be like desecrating a grave to move him from the place where he had been for so long.

Stop it! Stop conjecturing, she told herself. You'll have to wait and see what happens, and in the meantime you're not alone. Daniel will help you through this.

As she went towards Pinocchio Ward Helen could hear the deep murmur of his voice as the sister escorted him around the beds. She was desperate to see him, speak with him, but first there was a new admission in Pluto that she had to see: a four-year-old mite whom she'd seen in Outpatients because of recurring bronchial problems, and now the little girl had been admitted with suspected pneumonia. A chest X-ray had already been taken showing consolidation of various parts of the right lung, and after a throat swab and blood culture she was about to prescribe treatment once she'd seen the child.

'I'm putting her on intravenous benzylpenicillin,' she told the bright-eyed young nurse standing beside her.

As she started to write, the whiteness of the paper

seemed dazzling, as white as the Baltoro glacier from where K2 sprouted in cruel splendour. With an effort of will Helen calmed herself, finished the instructions, and told the nurse who was watching her curiously, 'I'll be back in a few moments.'

But her way to Pinocchio Ward was blocked by Jalal, sitting at the ward table with a game, his dark eyes appealing, and there was no way Helen could pass him without a word.

As she perched on the end of his bed the nurse who had been in attendance scuttled past with an anxious furtive look in her direction and Helen looked after her, puzzled. What was all that about? she wondered.

She was soon to find out. Within seconds Daniel was in the doorway, and as the shadows around her lifted at the sight of him she saw immediately that there was no joy on his part. He looked tense and angry. Mr Sunshine had been blotted out by a dark cloud for some reason.

'I need to speak to you,' he said curtly.

Helen sprang up quickly, alarm bells ringing inside her.

'Yes. What is it?'

The nurse had come back and was hovering just within earshot.

'What the hell do you think you're playing at?' he flared.

She stared at him. 'I don't understand.'

'You've just been prescribing for the child with pneumonia?'

'Yes.'

'Well, get the decimal point in the right place in future. If the nurse hadn't noticed your error, the child could have been severely overdosed!'

Helen gripped the end of Jalal's bed for support. Her

knees were buckling, and if she'd had a mirror she would have seen that her face was the whitest thing the morning had produced.

The disquiet that had started the day with her parents' early morning visit was expanding into a nightmare with every second. She didn't make that kind of mistake. . . not Helen Blake. But she had, hadn't she? Remorse washed over her in a sickly tide, and with it was the knowledge that it was she who was open to censure. . . not Daniel.

His face was hard and uncompromising, and if his anger had been directed at anyone else Helen might have been pleased to see that he could get tough if the occasion warranted it, but in that moment she was at her most vulnerable. . .she needed him to hold her close, and tell her that if it *was* Adam they found it would be just a shell, that his spirit was long gone.

But here he was berating her as if she were some first-year medical student, and Helen knew that, guilty or not, if she didn't gather her wits she would make an even bigger fool of herself by weeping in front of him.

'Can I leave you to make the necessary alteration?' he asked testily.

'Yes, you can,' she said grimly, fighting back. Her eyes went to the nurse who had turned away, pink-cheeked with embarrassment. 'I'd told the nurse I would be back in a moment, and then I would have done what I always do: checked my figures.'

'So you left the job half done to talk to the lad?'

No! she wanted to cry. I left it half done because I was desperate to see *you*! But instead she said frostily, 'I left the patient for a second, yes, but. . .'

'I really don't want to listen to you justifying yourself, Helen,' the tight-lipped stranger said. 'All I know is that

one of our small patients was about to be over-prescribed, and it won't do. We both know there has to be
room for human error, but I would never have expected
it of *you*.'

She could have screeched at him that it wasn't every
day she was told that her former fiancé's body had been
found, and maybe he might have understood, but he'd
just told her he wanted to hear no self-justification from
her, and his castigation *was* deserved. *She* would have
acted in just the same way had the boot been on the
other foot.

He was turning to go and the nurse was hurrying back
to her patients as she said bitterly, 'How dare you
address me like that in front of someone else? Hugh
Copley would have taken me into the office.'

The anger seemed to drain from him suddenly and he
brushed his hand wearily across his eyes, but there was
still no friendliness in his voice as he said, 'Yes, I
suppose he would but I care more about my little dolly
mixtures than hospital protocol.'

That really brought her out fighting. 'And I suppose
you think that I don't!'

'I don't know what I think,' he said defeatedly, as if a
huge burden had suddenly fallen on to his shoulders.
'But I'm amazed that a minor dispute between us should
affect your efficiency.'

'Don't flatter yourself,' she hissed angrily. 'It's taken
more than that to put me in the state I was in earlier.'

Daniel frowned, and there was a question in the
bright blue eyes. 'I don't get you,' he said.

'No, you don't, do you?' she slammed back. 'You're
too busy condemning me, which is not without its funny
side, as it's usually I who am trying to ignore *your*
shortcomings.'

On that sour note she turned her back on him and made her way to the bedside of the young pneumonia patient.

'I'm sorry I didn't show you the mistake first,' the nurse said uncomfortably. 'But you didn't seem yourself. That was why I took it to Mr Reed.'

Helen managed a smile. 'That's all right. You did what you had to do.' And as she made the alteration to the prescribed amount of benzylpenicillin Helen thought miserably that her world had well and truly fallen off its axis.

The moment she had finished on the wards Helen hurried off, striding out purposefully along the corridor with hands tightly clenched in the pockets of her coat. When she reached the nursing manager's office she marched in and sank down on to a chair.

Janice looked up from the paperwork on her desk, and when she saw her friend's face she got to her feet in alarm. 'You look awful, Helen,' she said. 'What's wrong?'

'Everything, Janice,' she said bleakly. 'I almost did a dreadful thing. I over-prescribed for one of the new admissions, and the nurse reported it to Daniel Reed before I'd had a chance to check the dosage. He's just made mincemeat out of me.'

'That doesn't sound like our happy-go-lucky senior consultant,' Janice said in surprise. 'And it doesn't sound like you either, Helen. You're one of the most efficient doctors I've ever met.'

'Not today, Jan,' she said sadly. 'Apart from Hugh Copley, you're about the only one at St Margaret's who remembers my engagement to Adam Kerwin, so you'll understand why I was absolutely shattered when I heard this morning that they may have found his body. It was an awful shock and it made me feel quite ill.'

Janice's face was full of concern. 'No wonder you weren't on form! Does Danny Boy know about this?'

'No, and I don't want him to. It doesn't alter the fact that I made a mistake, and until I can come to terms with that I shall be giving him a wide berth.'

'There'll be more than one climber lost on K2, you know,' Janice observed, returning to the subject of Adam.

'Yes, I know,' Helen agreed sombrely. 'My father is going to make enquiries and as soon as he has any news he'll be in touch. It was just a minor item on the early news this morning. I don't imagine it will make the later bulletins.'

'I think you should take the rest of the day off,' the nursing manager suggested. 'After all, you've had two major upsets this morning.'

Three, Helen thought grimly, and losing Daniel's good opinion was the biggest. 'No. I don't want him to have the satisfaction of thinking he's affected me that much.'

'But he has, hasn't he?' Janice said softly. 'From the way he looks at you I would have thought there was something between you.'

'There was, or at least *I* thought there was,' Helen said morosely, 'but it's past tense, I'm afraid, and that young madam Jill Morrison has something to do with it.'

'Really?' Her friend's eyebrows were arches of surprise.

'Why so amazed?' Helen asked. 'She's very attractive.'

'Yes, if you like that type,' Janice agreed doubtfully,

'but I heard Daniel Reed giving her a right ticking-off this morning, and she didn't like it one little bit.'

Helen stared at her. 'About the job?'

'No. It sounded more personal. He was telling her in no uncertain terms not to make assumptions about him.'

That might have been music to her ears earlier, but now it was just a sad lament and Helen didn't want to hear it.

The day passed with ward rounds in the morning and a big Outpatients' clinic in the afternoon, and now Helen had herself under control. Personal matters had been shelved, the needs of St Margaret's came first, and when it came to dotting the 'I's and crossing the 'T's. . . *and putting in the decimal points*. . .she didn't put a foot wrong.

She had put the nightmare of the dreadful mistake out of her mind. It would have to be faced, but when she was alone and in a calmer state of mind. Mistake it *had* been, pure and simple, and, even though she was positive she would have noticed it before the treatment began, the feeling of inadequacy and guilt was still there.

Her attitude when she'd had to speak to Daniel had been calm and professional, giving no hint of the hurt inside her, or the unspoken vow to put her heart back into the cold storage of non-involvement.

For his part he had been distantly polite, watching her with a sort of grim puzzlement, and she had wondered painfully if his hurt was as great as hers.

When it was time to go home Helen was first out, and by the time Daniel came strolling through the big swing doors her red Golf was already disappearing. Somehow or other she'd got through the day and now she couldn't wait to get home to lick her wounds.

She had needed his presence that morning more than mere words could express, but he hadn't tuned into her need. He'd been so incensed at what she'd done that he hadn't realised the state she was in, and what had been a small crack in their relationship the night before was now a huge chasm.

As she put her key in the lock the phone was ringing and when she picked it up her father's voice came over the line. 'I've been on to the Pakistani Consulate,' he said, 'and they tell me that their army have gone to bring the body in, but it could be days before there's any news. It depends on the weather and how difficult it is to reach, and so it's a matter of waiting, Helen, I'm afraid.'

'Yes, I see,' she said slowly, 'and thanks, Dad.'

'Whatever for, my dear?' he said huskily.

'For getting the information. . .and for being there for me, both you and Mum.'

'We're only too sorry this has happened. Like you, we prefer Adam to stay in the place he loved best, but we'll see what happens, eh?'

'Yes, we'll do that,' she agreed wearily.

Helen made a meal but she couldn't eat it, and, miserable and lonely, she went into the garden. Voices drifted over from the park, laughter, shouting, the cries of children, and her thoughts went to the house at the other side.

Thomas and Jonathan would be preparing for bed at this time, and if Bruno was still away their censorious father would be supervising bathtime. What wouldn't she give to be there with them, splashing and laughing, drying their small bodies with a huge soft towel. . .part of the young family that she'd never had.

It was unfair to call Daniel censorious, she thought

bleakly. He had merely been doing his job properly. . .
and *she* hadn't.

You're never satisfied, Helen Blake, she told herself.
When Daniel's Mr Nice Guy you disapprove, and you
like it even less when he takes you to task. You
shouldn't have set such store on an encounter by a
moonlit lake.

As she sat listlessly among the summer flowers the
gate clicked and hope rose in her, but it was Janice.

'I've come to see how you are,' she said with an
anxious smile.

'Wallowing in self-pity at the moment, I'm afraid,'
Helen confessed.

Janice put her arm around her shoulders. 'I think you
can be forgiven for that,' she said gently. 'Why don't
you come round to us for the evening? My terrible twins
would love to see you.'

'I'd be awful company.'

'It wouldn't matter,' the other woman persisted. 'I
don't like to think of you on your own with all this
misery inside you, Helen.'

Helen looked into her worried eyes and managed a
smile. 'Thanks for asking, Jan. You're a love, but I
really am better on my own. I need to be here in case
Dad has any more news for me.'

'All right,' Janice conceded reluctantly, 'but don't
forget that Aunty Jan always has a shoulder available to
cry on, even though she knows you'd prefer that of a
certain dishy senior consultant,' and as Helen smiled
weakly she went on, 'You're not going to let today's
mishap come between you, are you? If you really care
for the man, fight for him!'

'It's not just today,' she said slowly. 'It's the Jill

business as well. I think she sees herself as the future Mrs Reed and mother to his children.'

'Mother!' Janice hooted. 'She'd have them packed off to boarding-school the moment she got her foot in the door.'

'I couldn't bear the thought of that,' Helen breathed, 'and in any case Daniel wouldn't allow it.'

'No, I don't suppose he would,' her friend agreed. 'He's too kind and caring, and if he has any brains in his head he'll know that children flourish best in a happy family environment, and he'll also know that Jill Morrison is too young and brash to fit into that kind of situation.'

'And what about me?'

Janice grinned at her. '*You're* made for it, and for goodness' sake don't spoil it for you both because of foolish pride.'

It was a week before Helen and Daniel held any conversation that wasn't connected with St Margaret's, a week in which she'd gone about her duties in a state of frozen calm that thawed into misery once she got home.

The morning after the episode on Pluto Ward they had come face to face on the corridor, and after a quick glance at her set face his smile had faded and he'd just bade her a crisp, 'Good morning.'

She had acknowledged it briefly and continued on her way to Theatre, giving no sign that her heart had turned over at the sight of him. She had become aware halfway through the morning that there was no music coming from the theatre he was using, and she'd thought grimly that perhaps he hadn't switched on so that he'd be able to hear the screams of her patients were she to commit further misdemeanours.

Helen knew she was being childish. For one thing, Daniel didn't seem the type to bear a grudge. How had it all got out of hand like this? she'd asked herself a thousand times.

There had been no further news of Adam and Helen tried to push that particular nightmare to the back of her mind. As Janice had reminded her, other climbers had died on K2. It might be one of them, and someone else's sorrow.

'What ails our laughing consultant?' Mike Norton asked one morning in the staffroom. 'He seems to have lost his zest.'

'Perhaps he's feeling the pinch,' his friend John suggested. 'That old banger of his looks ready for the scrap heap, and I heard him telling someone the other day that he couldn't afford a new one.'

Helen had listened in perplexity. Daniel would have been joking, surely? His house was luxurious and spacious, and the children lacked for nothing. There was nothing about his lifestyle that indicated lack of cash, and yet his car *was* a bit decrepit. It had broken down on the morning of Jonathan's party, and he hadn't said anything about replacing it.

'Suppose he'll be out to make a fast buck on the foreign market, then, like the rest of 'em,' Mike had surmised, 'while us poor mortals slave away on the NHS.'

CHAPTER TEN

ON THURSDAY night her mother rang to say that she'd arranged a small dinner party for Saturday, and would Helen make sure she was free to attend?

No problem about that, she thought grimly. Her social life had suddenly become non-existent, and in her present mood she was prepared to let it stay that way, but as if Margaret was already anticipating a lack of enthusiasm she was in to the attack.

'I know that it's been a bad week for you, dear,' she said. 'You've never been out of our thoughts, but you know, even if it *is* Adam that they find out there on K2 it's not going to change anything, Helen. He is still dead, and *you* have to get on with your life.'

'Yes, I know that, Mum,' she said patiently, 'and I was doing just that, but this business of Adam has thrown me. Perhaps in a little while I'll feel better, but at the moment I'm really in the doldrums, and not just because of what's happening in Pakistan. There are other hurts I'm trying to cope with and they're not making me very sociable.'

'That's all the more reason to come,' her mother said briskly. 'It will be just our usual crowd, Janice and Ted, Hugh Copley, a couple of my staff from Rossiter, and the folks next door.'

'What about Jim Deardon? You usually invite him,' Helen said, as at the present time James's scowls and tantrums were definitely not on her list of things to be endured.

There was a pause and then Margaret said quickly, 'Yes, I know, but he's not been invited this time. As a matter of fact he's in Scotland for a few days, so will that persuade you to come? I believe you both went to see *Hiawatha* and parted company halfway through. He was telling your father.'

'Yes, we did. He was bored stiff and we ended up having a row.'

'Well, he won't be there to plague you on Saturday, so how about it?'

'Yes, of course I'll come,' she said, 'but don't expect me to be the life and soul of the party.'

'I won't,' her mother promised, and when she'd rung off Helen thought wryly that the dinner party would be for her benefit, to take her mind off Adam. But it wasn't on him, was it? It was besieged by thoughts of the man who had breezed into her life and turned it upside-down. The man with the put-together face, the quirky smile, and charm enough to bring the birds out of the trees, and who had just as much love for their profession as she had.

It was late on Friday afternoon and Helen was alone in the staffroom removing her doctor's garb when there was a knock on the door, and when she opened it she was surprised to find Bruno and the children standing there.

The young German smiled his dazzling smile and she felt a sudden rush of pleasure at the sight of them. These three were the part of the Reed household that she *could* cope with.

Thomas was clutching a crumpled envelope in his hand, and reminding her of the night when they'd brought the jogging-suit. Jonathan pushed him forward and said, 'Give it to Helen, Thomas,' and as his younger brother obeyed he said, 'It's a thank-you letter for the presents you gave us. I've written it and Thomas has put his name at the bottom next to mine.'

'I see,' she said gravely. 'I'd better read it, then.'

As her eyes went over the simple words written in a young child's unformed hand two pairs of bright blue eyes were fixed on her unblinkingly, so like their fathers that the dull ache inside her, which had eased a little when she'd seen them standing in the corridor, came back with renewed force.

'Is it all right?' Jonathan asked. 'Daddy said I had to do my best writing.'

'Yes, of course,' she breathed. 'It's lovely. I shall keep it in my purse.'

'The children have been asking when you are coming to the house again,' Bruno said, 'but I am telling them that you are the very busy doctor like their father.'

Helen's smile was tinged with sadness. She wouldn't be going to Daniel's house again unless she was invited, and the prospects of that looked remote at the present time, but she wasn't going to inflict her misery on his children, and so she said sincerely, 'I *am* busy, but not too busy for Thomas and Jonathan. Perhaps we can get together soon.'

'And me?' Bruno asked, his eyes warming, and reminding her uncomfortably of his ardour on the night they'd gone out.

'I suppose I'd have to put up with you,' she said lightly, 'as you're part of the package.'

'Is that all?' he pleaded with a grin.

'Yes, it is,' Helen said firmly, 'so don't go getting any ideas.'

As she was reaching for her coat the phone rang and

when she picked it up a youthful voice said, 'Is that Dr Blake?'

'Er. . .yes. Who's that?'

'It's Joanne.'

Helen's face brightened. 'Hello, Joanne. How are you?'

'Smashing, Doctor. I like it at my grandma's and I'm going to a new school. . .and the girls there are really nice.'

'I'm so pleased to hear that,' she said warmly. 'And are you eating well?'

'Yes. I'm always hungry now.'

'That's lovely, and I'm so pleased you've phoned, Joanne.'

'Can I ring you again some time?'

'Yes, of course. Whenever you want to.'

'That was one of the good moments of the job,' she told Bruno when she'd finished speaking to Joanne, 'and it wasn't due to medicine, just a bit of common sense.

'How's the leg?' she asked as they went outside.

'Better. Much better. I have not the pain now.'

'I can give you a lift if you like. It will save you walking.'

'Yes, that would be good,' he replied promptly. 'Then I shall have the food prepared before Daniel comes home from his private clinic.'

As she pulled away from the bottom of Daniel's drive Helen gave a gasp of dismay. The old black Rover was coming towards her. She felt her face go hot. The last thing she wanted was for him to find her on his doorstep.

When they drew level he stopped and she had no choice but to do the same. They eyed each other warily through the open car windows and Helen hoped that she wasn't responsible for the weariness in the face that was usually so untroubled.

She was the first to speak. 'Bruno and the children called in at St Margaret's with a thank-you note, and I gave them a lift home,' she explained stiffly.

Daniel's face softened into the beginning of a smile. 'It took Jonathan a long time to produce that.'

She smiled back. It appeared they could discuss the children without constraint. 'Yes, I'm sure it did. I shall treasure it.'

'You will?' he said absently as his eyes went slowly over her face and the slender throat where a pulse flickered. 'It's nice to know that all my family aren't out of favour.'

'Thomas and Jonathan are delightful,' she parried back, 'but then they don't have doubts about my competence,' and immediately thought that a disruptive demon was putting words into her mouth.

'Neither do I,' Daniel said unsmilingly. 'I've realised since that something was very wrong that morning on Pluto Ward, but as you don't seem to be prepared to discuss it I suppose that's it.'

Helen shifted in her seat. They were behaving like polite strangers when she ached to touch him, to trace the craggy lines of his face with tender fingers, to feel the strength and fire of him in her arms. . .but the fire had gone out, hadn't it? The spark had never had the chance to become a flame.

He was moving off and the weariness was back in his face. 'Bye for now, Helen. Thanks for bringing my family home.'

* * *

On Saturday night Helen dressed for her mother's dinner party with extreme care. She'd been less than enthusiastic when Margaret had broached the subject, and now she felt that she owed it to her parents to look and act alive, as she was pretty sure they were organising it for her benefit.

She chose a low-necked dress of sea-green silk that clung to the firm globes of her breasts and then fell straight to her knees, from where it flared around her legs at mid-calf. With it she wore silver jewellery, long drop earrings with a single green stone in them and a delicate choker necklace around her throat.

She looked elegant and very beautiful in the dress, but when she studied her face in the mirror it was pale and there were dark smudges beneath her eyes. So much for love, she thought. . .an overrated experience.

'You look lovely, dear,' her mother said softly when she arrived, and in an even lower voice, 'Still no news, I'm afraid.'

'I realise that, Mum,' Helen said flatly, 'or one of you would have been on the phone.'

Margaret's keen eyes went over her daughter's white face. 'Yes, well, tonight we'll forget what's gone, shall we, and concentrate on what's to come?'

'Yes, of course,' Helen agreed, while wondering what all that was about.

When she went into the sitting-room Helen found Janice and her husband Ted chatting to Hugh Copley and when the retired consultant saw her his face lit up.

'Helen! Good to see you, my dear,' he said heartily. 'How are you getting along with Daniel?'

Behind him Janice grimaced at the untimely question, and Helen wondered what the old man would say if she were to tell him that she was in love with Daniel Reed, that she couldn't eat, sleep, or concentrate for thinking about him, but she wasn't sure how he felt about her, as a certain young house officer that *he* had frowned upon kept turning up in his company.

Instead she told him with generous honesty, 'He's good, Hugh. . .very good, and totally committed. I've had to adjust to his ways, which are very different from yours, but as far as St Margaret's is concerned I think that the hospital is lucky to have him.'

He nodded, satisfied. 'That's good, because Daniel has a lot on his plate, not least being left with two small children to bring up alone. Have you met them?'

'Er. . .yes. . . I have. We introduced ourselves by the lake in Linnias Park,' she said with a smile, 'when one of them fell in.'

Hugh Copley stared at her. 'Really?' He wrinkled his nose in distaste. 'That would be rather messy.'

Helen laughed. 'It was, believe me!' And nothing has been straightforward since, she wanted to add.

Her father was looming up with a tray of drinks and he raised an enquiring eyebrow. 'You all right, love?'

'Yes, Dad,' she told him, her heart twisting. He and her mother never pushed themselves on to her, but they were always there for her, and Helen knew that when she hurt so did they.

Their next-door neighbours, a young couple in their thirties, came breezing up at that moment and the conversation became general.

The other two members of the party, women teachers from Rossiter Comprehensive, gave a friendly wave from the depths of the sofa, and Helen thought that the combination of delicious smells coming from the kitchen and the fact that all the guests were present indicated that they would soon be eating.

When she went into the dining-room she saw that eleven places had been set and there were only ten of them. Obviously her mother had forgotten to mention someone, or she'd miscounted. Perhaps she'd invited an extra man to offset herself and the lady teachers.

The thought had no sooner entered her mind than Helen had a feeling that she might just know who the extra place had been set for. Jim Deardon was in Scotland, so he was out of the way, but someone else wasn't, was he? *He* was close by.

Yes, he was close by all right. Her father had just opened the door to him and Daniel was striding into the hall, holding a spray of pale pink roses and looking happy and relaxed.

Helen whizzed into the kitchen and found her mother, rosy-cheeked, lifting a golden turkey out of the oven.

'Mother! How could you?' she whispered fiercely. 'Why didn't you tell me that you'd invited Daniel?'

Her mother placed the roasting tin carefully on the unit and then looked her squarely in the eye. 'I didn't tell you because I thought you wouldn't come. I'd guessed there is some friction between you.'

'Right in one,' she snapped.

'But why?' Margaret asked. 'What's the man done to you?'

'Nothing, except make me miserable and confused. I was better off before I knew him; at least I knew what I was doing, and where I was going.'

'Rubbish!' Margaret whispered, with a furtive look towards the door to make sure they were still alone. 'Before you met Daniel Reed you weren't living. . .you were existing. If you want this man, for goodness' sake do something about it.'

That was what Janice had said. 'Fight for him.' But that night when they'd watched *Hiawatha* together, surrounded by magic and an exhilarating awareness of each other, it had all seemed so right that friction and confusion had been the furthest things from her mind.

'So here you both are,' he said from the doorway. 'My hostess and her beautiful daughter.' Daniel went up to Margaret and, placing the flowers in her arms, he kissed her gently on the cheek, and with his eyes on Helen standing stiffly beside her he said with a wicked gleam in his eye, 'Thanks for inviting me, Mrs Blake. My social life seems to be on a downward spiral.'

Helen saw that the weariness of yesterday had left him and he was back to his usual unruffled self. He was wearing a white shirt with a brightly patterned tie and dark blue trousers. He looked cool and immaculate with the springing gold of his hair brushed flat, and, catching her appraising glance, he smiled his devastating smile.

'I broke my own record today. It only took me ten minutes to iron the shirt.'

His mood was catching and Helen's spirits lifted. 'Why? How long does it usually take?' she asked.

'Depends on how enthusiastic I am.'

Margaret was shooing them out of the kitchen. 'Go and introduce Daniel to the folks he doesn't know, Helen, while I dish up,' she suggested.

He was seated next to her during the meal and Helen watched with tender amusement how he seemed to be the focal point of the gathering without any effort on his part, or awareness that he was. Daniel had the looks and personality to charm people. . .and make hearts beat faster if her own was anything to go by.

Each time he turned to speak to her their eyes were only inches apart and she knew it was there again, the nearness, the chemistry between them. She was a fool ever to think it had gone.

'I need to talk to you when we get a moment to ourselves,' he said in a low voice when they were unobserved.

The beautiful hazel eyes widened. She felt reckless and excited. 'What is it? Tell me now.'

Daniel shook his head and laughter glinted in his eyes. 'Such impatience, Minnehaha.'

Colour flooded her face. So he hadn't forgotten.

'I'll give you a clue,' he offered, tuning into her mood.

She laughed up at him. 'Animal, vegetable, mineral. . .or a truce?'

He adopted a thoughtful pose. 'Now let me see. . .a truce, I think; yes, definitely a truce.'

Happiness filled her, and, catching her mother's eyes upon her, Helen smiled her thanks. Margaret had thrown them together tonight in the hope that they would sort out their differences and it looked as if her plan might succeed.

Lost in the pleasure of her thoughts, Helen wasn't at first aware that Hugh Copley was speaking to her across the table, and when she tuned in to what he was saying she froze with dismay.

'They said on the early evening news that it *is* Adam Kerwin's body they've found on K2. Strange after all this time, isn't it? Am I right in thinking he was an acquaintance of yours, Helen?'

She saw the consternation on her mother's face and heard her father's gasp of dismay, but she was more concerned with the reaction of the man beside her.

Helen saw surprise and then the dawning of understanding in his eyes, and her throat went dry. Every time she and Daniel seemed to be getting close they were diverted, either by the living. . .or the dead; and as the shock of what she'd just been told began to sink in, desperate for a breathing space, she got to her feet, and, excusing herself in a shocked whisper, hurried through the French windows into the garden.

When she'd gone as far as she could Helen stopped and, holding on to a slender tree-trunk, stood motionless with bent head. The night was dark and starless and very warm, yet she felt cold, and knew it was because the hand of death had reached out across the miles and the years and touched her again.

Hugh Copley's timing had been dreadful, unintentionally so, but dreadful nevertheless. Obviously he was completely unaware of just how close she and Adam had been, and, fond of her in his own dry way, he would never have brought the subject up in public if he'd known.

Helen knew that her parents would be just as devastated as she, but they had a room full of guests, and also they would know that she needed to be alone for the first few moments as she faced up to what had happened.

What was Daniel thinking back there? she wondered. He had a past himself but there were no loose ends to it. He'd loved someone and her life-span had been short like Adam's, but that had been it. In her own case, echoes were coming back over the years and she didn't want it to be like that, she thought raggedly.

She'd often wished to know where Adam really was, but now, when it looked as if her wish might be granted, she knew that she didn't want his body disturbed out there among the everlasting snows. He wouldn't want his final resting place to be in some suburban churchyard.

Why, oh, why, did they have to find him just at this time? When her life was taking shape again.

'So that's what it was all about?' Daniel said quietly from behind. 'Why you weren't your usual self on Monday morning?'

Helen nodded mutely.

'Why didn't you tell me?'

The stress inside made her swing round on him in quick anger. 'I was going to. I was desperate to tell you, but I didn't get the chance, did I?'

'No, you didn't,' he admitted. 'The little nurse was bending my ear before the mistake had even happened.'

'No, Daniel, that's not true,' she said defeatedly. 'The kid was only doing her job. The error *had* been made, but thankfully hadn't been acted upon.

'Apparently they had said on the early morning news on Monday that they might have found Adam. I hadn't heard it, but my parents had, and they came round to tell me. It came as a great shock after all this time.'

'You loved him a lot?'

'Yes, I did.'

It was true, she had loved him very much, but now it seemed like a mere youthful crush compared to how she felt about Daniel, and at the first opportunity she would tell him so, but for now all she wanted was for him to take her in his arms and soothe away her misery and panic, tell her that none of it mattered as long as they had each other. But he didn't. Instead he took her hand and looking down on the slender ringless fingers he said, 'Who is going to have to make the decision about moving Kerwin? Has he any close relatives?'

'No. None,' she said bleakly.

'So supposing they ask you, Helen? What will you

say? Would you want to go out to Kashmir to see them bring him in?'

She shuddered. 'No. If I have any say in it I want him left where he is. That's what he would want. Adam had two close friends who were part of the same British expedition on which he was lost. I shall contact them to see what they advise.'

'Yes, do that,' he agreed, 'and in the meantime if *I* can do anything to help don't hesitate to ask.'

His voice was kind, polite, the voice of a friend rather than a lover. The delicious promise of the night had shrivelled like a pricked balloon. Perhaps he felt that a sort of restrained dignity was called for in the circumstances, but Helen wanted to cry to him that she needed him, needed his strength and love now just as much as she'd needed it that day on Pluto.

'Let me take you home, Helen,' he suggested. 'It will only make matters worse if you have to listen to Copley apologising for his clanger.'

'Yes, all right,' she agreed dismally.

'Stay where you are,' he ordered, 'and I'll go back inside and explain to your parents.'

She nodded, and as he moved quickly through the velvet night Helen put her head in her hands and wept.

When Daniel came back she was sniffling into a small white handkerchief, and after a long, compassionate look he fished a clean white square out of his pocket. 'They're much easier to iron than a shirt,' he said with a smile, 'so weep all you want. There's no shame in weeping over someone we love.'

Face blotchy and eyes red-rimmed, Helen looked at him over the big handkerchief. She loved him so much that her very bones were melting with longing, but his attitude was making it quite clear that once again it wasn't the right time or place.

When they got back to the cottage, Daniel said briskly, 'Go upstairs, get undressed, and into bed,' and as her eyes widened, 'This is your doctor speaking, Miss Blake, not someone who is about to ravish you on your virginal bed.'

'Why are you taking it for granted that I'm a virgin?' she asked listlessly with one foot on the bottom stair.

'Just a certain magical aura,' he said with a smile.

'Not the aura of the frigid spinster, then?'

'No, never that,' he declared firmly, 'and now that we've clarified your status in the sex charts perhaps you'll do as you're told. . .get into bed and I'll bring you a hot drink.'

'Yes, Daniel,' she said meekly, and knew that she'd no wish to argue.

He sat beside her as she drank the warm Horlicks he'd brought up, his eyes on her shadowed face, the smooth skin of her neck and shoulders, and the soft mounds of her breasts in a short cotton nightgown.

There was no desire in his brilliant blue gaze. If there was any emotion in him Helen would have said it was sadness, and she thought guiltily that she was making Daniel miserable with her problems.

When she'd finished the drink she lay back on the pillows and looked up at him and as their glances held he said decisively, 'You've had a nasty shock. Take it easy tomorrow—a day in bed perhaps?'

Helen raised herself up on to one elbow in protest. 'I'll be all right, Daniel, really I will.'

He was eyeing her doubtfully. 'Are you sure?'

'Yes, I'll feel better in the morning. Everything seems simpler in the light of day.'

He still wasn't happy. 'Well, if you say so, but I'm off to London in the morning to meet a friend and may not have time to check on you unless I ring very early.'

His concern was balm to her fraught nerves. 'Don't worry,' she told him gently. 'I'm already adjusting, and this news doesn't really change anything. My feelings about Adam haven't altered.'

'No, I don't suppose they have,' he said sombrely, 'and I don't suppose they ever will.'

There was a note of defeat in his voice that really worried her, but even as she puzzled over it Daniel was kissing her gently on the brow and taking his leave, and as he went she wondered miserably whether there would ever be a right time for them.

When he'd gone she fell asleep, suddenly and deeply, but only for a short time and then she was awake again, going over in her mind all that had happened in the last few hours.

It was dawn before Helen closed her eyes a second time and now her sleep was plagued with weird dreams. She was searching for Daniel, desperately climbing a snow-covered mountain, and each time she caught a glimpse of him he was gone by the time she caught up. Then the mountain became a huge pile of dolly mixtures and he was standing at the top looking down, but every time she moved towards him on the brittle candies it was like walking on shale and she slipped back.

When she awoke again she was covered in perspiration, and as she lay staring at the ceiling she wondered if the dream had been anything to do with the look in Daniel's eyes when he'd left her.

The phone rang as she was preparing breakfast, and when she picked it up a flat Yorkshire voice that she hadn't heard in years spoke in her ear.

'Helen?'

'Yes,' she answered warily.

'Greg Latham here. Remember me?'

'Well, yes, of course I do. You're Adam's friend,' she said quickly.

'I've been on to your parents and they gave me this number. I believe you're aware that they've found Adam?'

'Yes, I am,' she said carefully. 'I was going to ring *you*, but you've beaten me to it.'

'I thought you might be in touch,' he said. 'It's a bit awkward with Adam having no folks, isn't it?'

'Yes,' Helen agreed, with the feeling that she'd like to know what Greg thought before she voiced any opinions.

'I'm actually in Kashmir now,' he was explaining. 'I only heard that he'd been sighted yesterday and I flew right out. I'd like to have been with the search party, least I could do for a best mate, but I was too late.

'The army have sent a message back that he's been preserved in the ice and is in a very recognisable state, but they've still got to get across a dangerous crevasse to move him and want instructions from next of kin as to what they've got to do.

'As he's got no blood kin, Joe and I thought it should be up to you. So what do you think? Do you want to come out here?'

'No,' she said decisively. 'I don't. I think Adam should be left where he is, in the place where he was happiest. It's what he would want, but I *would* like to know what you and Joe Goodison think.'

'We agree with you,' he said without hesitation. 'Adam wouldn't want to be a peep-show in some Kashmir morgue, and I'm pretty sure the authorities will agree that it's more respectful to leave him where he is, and thereby also reduce the hazards for the soldiers who've been sent out there. If you want to leave it with me I'll pass on your comments. Has this upset you?' he asked awkwardly. 'It's a bit of a facer after all this time, isn't it? Especially if you've made other relationships.'

'I have, but only just,' she told him, 'and somehow that seems to make it worse. It's a precious new affection and I don't want it spoiled because of this.'

'I don't blame you for feeling like that,' he said gravely. 'Adam did what *he* wanted with his own life, and you're entitled to do the same with yours, Helen. You had a raw deal, and if you have the chance of happiness take it, and leave the other business to me.'

When he had gone off the line Helen's spirits lifted. Although he was just as obsessed with mountaineering as Adam had been, Greg Latham was prepared to admit that his friend hadn't been fair to her, and she knew that she *was* going to take his advice, without any shadow of a doubt.

The sweet chemistry between Daniel and herself had been there again last night. He had been at his most heart-stopping, tender, amusing, attractive, making her pulse race, and then Hugh Copley had poured cold water on their enchantment.

He had ended up treating her with a resigned sort of compassion that had frightened rather than comforted her, and tomorrow, if not tonight, she was going to tell him how she felt about him: how she loved him from the deepest core of her being; how other men, past and present, had ceased to have any meaning for her since she'd met him.

She rang the house in the late evening and when she

asked for Daniel was told by Bruno that he wasn't back.
'He will be late, I think, Helen,' he said. 'He has gone
to meet his friend, Lars, who is in England for a short
visit on medical business. Daniel said they would have
much to discuss.'

'So his friend is a doctor too,' she said thoughtfully.

'Yes, it is so. Will I not do instead of Daniel?' he
asked soulfully. 'I am lonely now that the boys are in
bed.'

She laughed. 'Too bad. You'll have to find yourself a
good book. . .as I'm going to do.'

CHAPTER ELEVEN

MONDAY morning came and went. It was lunchtime and Daniel hadn't appeared. Helen knew there could be various reasons why, such as an emergency regarding a private patient, a management meeting, or a resources discussion. . .or after yesterday he might have just slept late. . .but whatever it was, she wished he would appear and put her world to rights.

She had done her ward rounds, examined new admissions who were to be in her charge, sanctioned the discharge of Sharon the minibus victim, and the small pneumonia sufferer, both of whom would be attending Outpatients until she was satisfied with their progress, and was having a quick cup of coffee when Janice appeared.

'Poor you. . .and poor old Hugh,' she said ruefully, 'and hard luck on the delightful Daniel who is obviously well smitten.'

Helen nodded bleakly. 'Yes, some fiasco, wasn't it? And I have yet to confirm the smitten part of it.'

'No? That's because you weren't sitting where I was,' the nursing manager said with a smile, and then becoming serious again, 'Hugh Copley was mortified when he discovered just how close you'd been to Adam Kerwin. Obviously if he'd known he would have kept quiet, but I sensed that your mum and dad were happy enough to leave you in the care of our doctor friend.'

'He took me home and put me to bed with a cup of Horlicks.'

'He's a lovely man. He can tuck me in any time,' Janice retorted.

'Yes, he is,' Helen agreed, 'but I have this feeling that he thinks I'm in love with a memory.'

Janice eyed her thoughtfully. 'I might have thought that myself at one time, but not now, not since you met Daniel Reed. When you're near him there is that unmistakable glow about you.'

Helen sighed. 'It's merely a glimmer at the moment, but once he puts in an appearance I'm going to clear the air between us.'

Helen was sharing a table in the staff dining-room with Mike and John when she saw Daniel go past, and the moment she'd finished her meal she went to his office.

His eyes warmed when he saw her standing there, and then they became cautious. 'Hello, and how are you?' he asked gently.

The exquisite pleasure of seeing him again was making her feel weak. 'Much better, thank you. I've sorted out my thoughts. . .and my priorities.'

He became still. 'You have?' He sighed and glanced at his watch. 'That word has cropped up twice in the last five minutes.'

'What do you mean?'

'We have one here at St Margaret's. It's just been passesd on to me, and I suggest we deal with it together.'

Helen groaned inwardly. That was exactly what she'd had in mind, a joint tackling of priorities, but not connected with the hospital.

'What is it?' she asked weakly.

'I've just had a call from Neo-natal to say that over the weekend one of their infants was shown to have oesophageal atresia with a tracheo-oesophageal fistula, which means we're going to have to do a thoracotomy to ligate it.'

His eyes flicked over her face. 'And when it's over I need to talk to you.'

'That makes two of us,' she said on a rising tide of optimism. It *was* going to be all right. She knew it.

As they walked briskly down to Theatre Daniel said, 'I'd better fill you in. Case history is premature delivery, probably due to mother having polyhydramnios late in the pregnancy. Child all right at first but soon started frothing. Ward staff had no luck with either nasogastric or large-bore orogastric tubes because of the obstruction, so at the moment there's a double-lumen suction tube in the pouch.'

The team were ready and waiting, and as the operation commenced Helen felt the adrenalin start to flow. Surgery was a strange mixture of power and humility, a time when everything else was blotted out and the whole universe centred on those working beneath the harsh lights. It was their world, hers and Daniel's, and as she looked down on to the tiny inert figure on the table Helen prayed as always that their skills would be enough.

She watched Daniel's steady hand make an incision between the child's shoulderblades, and saw it curve round the side of the trunk to just below the nipple. Now he could get to the chest cavity and ligate the fistula, and once that had been done they placed a drainage tube into the pleural cavity to prevent the lung from collapsing. The child's heartbeat had remained regular throughout and as Helen stitched up the incision there was a slacking of the tension among them.

'We'll need to do a second repair in a few weeks' time,' Daniel told her as they cleaned up.

She nodded. 'Yes, to join the two ends of the oesophagus. I'd like to be in on that, too, if I may.'

He smiled. 'Of course. I like to have you near me. . . socially *and* professionally.'

That made her heart beat faster, but it slowed down as he said, 'But there's something I have to tell you first. Shall we go back to my office?'

As they walked back along the corridor Helen said, 'Did Bruno tell you that I rang last night?'

'Yes, he did.'

'I just wanted to let you know that I was all right, but of course you weren't back. He suggested that I went over to keep him company. . .said he was lonely.'

He laughed, but it wasn't his usual easy chuckle. 'Did he, now? The cheeky young blighter! I can handle him, though, *and* a chauvinistic red-haired GP if I have to. The living I can cope with. It's the dead that have me beat.'

Helen took a deep breath. This had to be it. . .the moment she'd been waiting for, but before *she* could say her piece Daniel was saying something else and it wiped her mind blank.

'I was late getting here this morning because I've been making travel arrangements, and I wanted to tell you before anyone else did. . . I'm going away, Helen.'

'Going away?' she echoed.

'Yes, I'm leaving the country in a couple of days and expect to be away for at least a week. The friend I saw yesterday has asked me to assist him with a heavy programme of surgery, and I've agreed. Bruno will look after the boys, of course, but I'd be grateful if you would look in on them when you get the chance.'

Helen was staring at him, dumbfounded. She was remembering Mike's words that day in the staffroom when he and John had been discussing Daniel's car, and she felt sick inside.

'So you *are* out to make a fast buck!' she said with the bitterness of disillusion, unconsciously using the young house officer's own words. 'I've heard of consultants going abroad, especially to places like Scandinavia, where they can command a fat fee while still being paid at this end, but I would never have thought it of *you*!'

The huge hazel eyes were sparking angry fire, but instead of flaring back at her he was looking at her in pained amazement, and when Helen stopped for breath he asked with a sort of weary tolerance, 'Have you quite finished?'

Finished. . .a very final sort of word, and in this moment of her outrage totally applicable. 'Yes, I have!' she slammed back at him.

As Helen drove home at the end of the day she was thinking grimly, so much for assuring Daniel that he was the only man for her, so much for the cosy family outing to *Winnie-the-Pooh*, and so much for the rosy future that had become daubed with shades of grey.

'How can he think of leaving Thomas and Jonathan . . .his small patients at St Margaret's. . .and me?' she wailed to the empty car. She had been kidding herself about his integrity and worth. Daniel Reed possessed strong chameleon-like tendencies that she should have had the sense to recognise before now.

His car might be an old wreck, but she was pretty sure it was because he was fond of it, not because he couldn't afford to replace it. A consultant of his standing, even with a family and the upkeep of a large house, would be far from penniless . . . so why. . .why. . .was he doing this thing?

* * *

As she ate her evening meal Helen was already experiencing the dissatisfaction of her alienation from Daniel, but in this instance on a professional basis.

She'd seen a baby in Outpatients that afternoon and needed his advice. The infant was showing the symptoms of something she hadn't come across before, but the odds were that Daniel had.

Obviously she wasn't going to let a personal matter affect the treatment of a child in her care, and she had reluctantly sought him out for an opinion, only to be told he had left early. Which meant she either spoke to him tonight, which was the last thing she wanted to do after the lunchtime bust-up, or hoped she could pin him down tomorrow which would be on his last day before he flew out to Scandinavia.

She decided that it would have to be tonight, but in the form of a phone call rather than a confrontation, and by doing it that way there would be no need for contact between them on the following day. If any other problems cropped up in his absence it would be just too bad, she thought grimly, but she would worry about that kind of thing when and if it happened.

'Reed here,' his warm, lazy voice said in her ear when she rang his home.

'It's Helen,' she said coldly. 'I'm sorry to disturb you but I need advice regarding an infant I saw this afternoon.'

'Oh, what a disappointment,' he said in amused mockery. 'I thought you were about to shower me with apologies.'

Anger raced through her again. 'The chances of that are just about as remote as me wishing you a good trip,' she snapped, 'but if you could spare a moment from your usual inanities I need to talk shop.'

He was immediately serious. 'Sorry, Helen. I should have realised that your sense of humour wouldn't be functioning after my dastardly behaviour. Go ahead, I'm listening.'

'I saw a young baby in Outpatients this afternoon that has been referred from the local health clinic. They were concerned that the infant had chronic constipation and little weight gain since birth. I examined him and was convinced it was something organic.

'The clinic had advised the mother not to feed him until he'd been seen by us and so we were able to give him a barium enema. It showed the large bowel very dilated, then narrowing into a small constricted segment. I haven't encountered it before but I wondered if it might be Hirchsprung's Disease.'

'Sounds like it,' he said thoughtfully. 'Have you had the child admitted?'

'Yes.'

'I'll see him in the morning, then, and if it is what we think I'll operate. It won't be the easiest surgery I've ever done. It will be a case of relieving the obstruction, followed by excision of the segment, and joining of the two ends of the normal intestine.'

'I see,' she said stiffly. 'That's what I needed to know. Thank you.' And before he could rile her any further she replaced the phone.

As she recalled his past tenderness Helen could hardly believe that Daniel could be so insensitive, but she'd just had proof of it, and she felt that he couldn't care less that her opinion of him was at rock-bottom. If tomorrow went by without their paths crossing that was fine by her.

It didn't. As Helen drove the red Golf into the hospital car park Daniel was just getting out of the

Rover, and her hands tightened on the wheel. She'd been awake most of the night trying to come to terms with what was happening to them, and was in no state for any further confrontation, but she needn't have worried; he gave a brief salute and strode off towards the main entrance.

They were both due in Theatre. Until the admission of the child they'd discussed on the phone, Daniel had only one operation on his list. If he diagnosed Hirchsprung's Disease then he would have two, whereas her own list was long enough to take most of the day, and Helen wasn't sorry about that if it kept them apart.

Jill Morrison was in the staffroom and she flashed Helen her confident smile. 'Hi, Helen. What's new?'

'Not a lot,' she replied steadily. 'What's new with you?'

'I've applied for a vacancy at a paediatric hospital in Bristol. Wish me luck, eh?'

Helen smiled. This was a turn-up for the book. 'Well, yes, of course I do. You've a lot of ability. You could go far, Jill.'

'Daniel suggested it. He'd heard there was an opening for someone like me there, and I love change.'

'Good luck, then,' Helen said as she digested the surprising fact that it was Daniel's idea for the glossy young blonde to move. If that man wasn't full of surprises she didn't know who was, and they weren't all nice ones, she thought glumly.

As Helen stepped out on to the corridor Daniel was coming towards her and she thought, So much for non-involvement. They'd already been within sighting distance twice and the day had hardly begun.

'I've examined the little one we discussed last night and seen the X-ray of the barium enema. It's as we thought: Hirchsprung's Disease. They're getting him ready for Theatre now. Do you want to assist?' he asked.

She would have dearly liked to say yes, but for various reasons she wasn't going to. She could just about endure the thought of what he had planned for the coming week if she kept out of his way, and assisting him in Theatre was hardly keeping out of Daniel's way. And another reason, far more logical, was the fact that she already had a very full day ahead of her without another item of surgery added to it.

'No, thanks,' she told him coolly, and strode past with a leisurely, measured stride that gave no hint of her inner misery.

The music was blaring forth defiantly as he operated and Helen thought that next week would be a time of silence, and the reason for it would be eating away at her. Before she might have been glad of it, but now there would be an awful feeling of emptiness as she worked in the theatre, no comforting thought that, music or not, Daniel was only a few feet away.

It had been a gruelling few hours of surgery and as she made her way wearily along the main corridor Daniel appeared once more, this time at the door of his office.

'Can you spare a minute?' he asked, motioning for her to go inside.

Helen nodded grimly. 'Yes. What is it?'

'I was wondering what you've decided regarding Kerwin. There doesn't seem to have been an opportunity to ask you,' he said, watching her carefully.

And whose fault is that? she felt like shrieking, but instead she told him frostily, 'One of his climbing friends rang me on Sunday morning. He was actually in Kashmir, and asked what my wishes were.'

'And?'

She took a deep breath. What was the point of all this? Whatever happened regarding Adam it made no difference now. Her brief idyll with Daniel had died almost at birth. She needn't have got herself into such a state, but he *had* been there when the news came through, and he'd been kind and caring, so courtesy demanded that she answer his question.

'I told him that if it was left to me I would want Adam to stay among the snows, and he said that he would pass my wishes on to the authorities. After all, that part of my life is over. I mourned him too long.'

Helen heard his quick intake of breath and saw a strange look in his eyes, and was angry with herself for letting him draw her into conversation, but he was planting himself firmly in front of her, blocking escape, and he said softly, 'You've made it plain that you're not going to say goodbye, which I suppose is all I deserve, but there's nothing to stop me bidding *you* a fond farewell, is there?' And his arms reached out, pulling her to him with a sudden desperate urgency that took her by surprise.

His kiss explored her lips gently at first and then began to possess them utterly, making her blood race and her heart pound in her breast. It was passionate, demanding, but with the bitter-sweetness of farewell, and when at last he let her go Daniel gave a deep sigh, but he was smiling his quirky smile as he suggested, 'When I get back we'll have a night on the town, eh, Helen, on the strength of my "fat fee"?' And, picking up his briefcase, he touched her lightly on her burning cheek and departed, leaving her bemused and furious.

*   *   *

'What's this about Danny Boy having jetted off to foreign lands?' Mike asked the next morning. 'It's been kept very quiet, hasn't it? Did you know he was taking leave, Helen?'

'Yes, he did mention it,' she said awkwardly.

He wasn't beating about the bush. 'Where's he gone, and what for?' the young doctor wanted to know.

'He'll be performing surgery in one of the Scandinavian countries, I presume.'

'I see, so their gain is our loss,' he pronounced in sepulchral tones, and Helen had to laugh, even though with regards to herself there was a large element of truth in the remark.

Through the day Helen's thoughts kept turning to Bruno and the children. Daniel had asked her to call on them if she got the chance, and, much as she resented his nerve, she was aware that *they* were innocent of any involvement in his machinations.

Perhaps a casual call on her way home, she decided. It wouldn't look too obvious, as if she was checking up on them, and yet it would put her mind at rest. Then maybe another quick call at the end of the week, though she was on duty all over the weekend. Following on from that she had three days off, and what she was going to do with them she hadn't decided.

Helen found them in the garden, the children playing with an assortment of toys scattered over the lawn, and Bruno watering the plants in the conservatory. It was a peaceful happy scene and her heart lifted. Nothing to worry about here, she thought thankfully.

When he saw her Bruno came out of the glasshouse, smiling with pleasure. 'Hello, Helen. What brings you here?'

'Just a neighbourly call,' she said easily. 'I wondered if you needed any help while Daniel is away.'

He shook his head. 'We're fine, thanks. He left everything organised for us. He did a big shop for us yesterday, so we are not short of food. I think we will be faring better than he.'

Helen gave a dry laugh. 'You must be joking! Tucked away in some swish Scandinavian clinic? He won't exactly be reduced to beans on toast.'

Helen could tell that Bruno wasn't following her. He was staring at her, puzzled. 'Daniel has gone to Bangladesh,' he said slowly. 'His friend, Lars, has been gathering together a team of paediatric surgeons to go out there and give their services, operating on children who have been injured in the chaos that the horrendous floods have brought. I feel that he will be fortunate if he has the time to eat.'

He was watching the colour drain from her face. 'I am surprised he didn't tell you. The only reason Daniel would ever leave his own children is to help little ones less fortunate.'

Helen felt her insides clench with dismay, and on legs that seemed to have become suddenly boneless she stumbled to a nearby garden chair and slumped down on to it.

Daniel *would* have told her if she'd given him the chance, but she hadn't, had she? She'd been so eager to condemn the man she loved that she hadn't given him the opportunity to show her that his kindness and generosity were limitless. What a self-righteous pain in the neck he must have thought her!

'Are you all right, Helen?' the young German was asking.

'Yes. . .yes, of course,' she said, forcing a smile. 'It's

just that I've had a very busy day. . .and the heat.' She got slowly to her feet. 'I'll be off, Bruno, and do please remember if there is anything at all I can do to help you have only to ask.'

When she got back to the cottage Helen went straight into the kitchen to make a cup of tea to calm her nerves, but, as she held the kettle under the tap, the tears that she'd been holding back ever since she'd left Bruno and the children came flooding, and as the kettle filled and then overflowed she wept out her remorse.

CHAPTER TWELVE

IF THERE was time to brood in her own home there was no opportunity to do so at St Margaret's during the next few days. With Daniel away, and small patients being admitted thick and fast, Helen and the three junior doctors were kept fully occupied, and she was thankful for it as it meant she was too tired to think when she got home in the evenings.

There had been no word from Bruno and she took it to mean that all was well at the house across the lake, but late Sunday evening the assumption was proved wrong. Helen had just showered before going to bed, and was curled on the settee with a mug of coffee, when the phone rang, and as soon as she heard the agitation in his voice she knew that Daniel's au pair had a problem.

'Helen! You said you would help, yes?' he said without preamble.

She sat up quickly. 'Yes, of course, Bruno. What's wrong? Is it the children?'

'No, they are all right.' His voice deepened with anxiety. 'It is my mother. She is very sick and I must go to her. Can you come to take care of Thomas and Jonathan, or I cannot go?'

'Yes. I'll get changed and be right over,' she said promptly. 'I've just finished a stint of duty so fortunately the next few days are free.'

The moment he had gone off the line she ran upstairs and packed a few clothes, and within minutes she was driving around the perimeter of the park to Daniel's house.

Bruno was waiting at the door looking pale and upset. 'Have you checked on flights?' she asked.

'Yes, there is a flight from Birmingham at three-thirty this morning, but how am I to get there?'

Helen thought a moment. She couldn't take him herself because of the children, but she knew someone who would.

'Hello, love,' her father said when he heard her voice on the phone. 'You've only just caught me. I was just about to have an early night.'

'Can you do me a favour, Dad?' Helen asked quickly. 'Well, it's a favour for someone else actually.'

'If I can. What is it?' he asked curiously. 'You sound a bit fraught.'

'I'll explain. Daniel has gone to Bangladesh to do some voluntary surgery and left the young German au pair in charge of the children.'

'Yes?'

'And Bruno has had an urgent message from home that his mother is very ill. I'm going to take over here — fortunately I've got a few days off — but the problem is that he has no car and needs to get to Birmingham Airport for half-past three to pick up a flight home.'

'Ah, now I comprehend,' he said. 'And you want *me* to take him?'

'If you would.'

'Well, of course I will,' and, unconsciously rubbing salt into her wounds, 'If a member of my profession is prepared to go out to operate among the dust and squalor in the aftermath of a disaster in Bangladesh, the least I can do is help out at this end. I'll be right over as soon as I've put your mother in the picture and checked that I'm all right for fuel.'

Her father was as good as his word and within quarter of an hour he was pulling up in front of the house. In the meantime Bruno had hurriedly packed his things, unearthed his passport, and was ready and waiting.

'Thank you for making it possible for me to go to my mother,' he'd said. 'I hope that Daniel will forgive me for rushing off like this, but I know that there is no one he would rather have care for his children than yourself.'

Helen had swallowed hard. In the light of recent events that was a dubious statement, but it had been said in all sincerity, and while her father was putting his luggage in the boot she gave Bruno a quick hug and said, 'I hope there is better news by the time you get home. Do let me know how things are if you get the chance.'

'I will do that,' he promised solemnly, and then with a quick wave of the hand he was running down the steps and they were away.

When he had gone the house felt strange and silent. She'd already looked in on the children and found them sleeping peacefully, but she went again to make sure that the noise of Bruno's departure hadn't disturbed them. However, all was well. Daniel's small sons were safe, and she intended to see that they remained so until he came back, which should be any time within the next few days, she reckoned.

There'd been no time to discuss sleeping arrangements with Bruno, and so the next thing Helen had to do was find somewhere to sleep. On investigation she found that the house had four bedrooms. One was occupied by the children, another left in some chaos as

Bruno's, the third looked as if it was intended as a guest room but there was no bed in it, and the fourth was Daniel's.

It was obviously the master bedroom, a large, airy room that looked across the park, and from the window she could see her own small abode outlined against the night sky. It was plainly furnished but with good taste: cream walls, a thick caramel-coloured carpet, warm oak furniture and a king-sized bed. It was charming and uncomplicated, like the man himself.

Helen grimaced at herself in the mirror. 'You've changed your tune,' she told herself. Not so long ago she'd had him as a devious chameleon type, and the shame of her behaviour still burnt within her, alongside a silent plea that she might be given the chance to ask his forgiveness or, as he'd suggested mockingly, shower him with apologies.

The bed sheets were of cream cotton, freshly laundered, but thrown on haphazardly, and as Helen straightened and tucked them in neatly her thoughts were far away, winging across the miles to where the man she loved was tending sick children in another land. Where would he be sleeping, she wondered, while she lay in his bed, if there was time for sleep?

A fresh breeze from the open window flattened her flimsy night gown against her long legs and firm buttocks, and lifted it away from her smooth thrusting breasts. There was an ache inside her, the ache of unfulfilment, the longing to feel Daniel's arms around her, his mouth on hers, his body possessing her.

The warm, scented night, the room, the bed, were all there; only the man was missing.

* * *

When the children awoke next morning it was amusing to watch them coming to grips with the fact that Bruno had changed into Helen overnight, but they loved the novelty of it and as they all breakfasted together Helen knew she could get to like the arrangement, as long as it was a foursome.

Bruno phoned in the early afternoon to say that he'd arrived home to find his mother improved, and once he was sure she was out of danger he would be back.

It wasn't the handsome au pair whom she was anxious to see return. He could stay away as long as he wished. It was Daniel she wanted to see, and the need was increasing with every second.

The children asked if they could have a picnic in the afternoon and Helen agreed, but with the proviso that it would have to be near the house in case Daniel should phone. So she carried a basket of food to the lakeside and, as they ate, the children fed the ducks that had come waddling over to investigate. Content to see them happy and engrossed, Helen was just biting into a potted-meat sandwich when she saw Jim Deardon approaching, hand in hand with the young receptionist from the surgery.

She turned away, but Jim's sharp eyes had already spotted her and he came over, leaving his companion beneath the shade of a clump of trees.

'Hello. What's going on here?' he asked in his usual abrupt manner.

'Nothing,' she told him blandly. 'Absolutely nothing. . .unless minding Daniel Reed's children counts as "something".'

'I'd say it does,' he said drily. 'I saw you with him that night in the park, you know, and it didn't take me long to work out why you were so lukewarm with me, but if a fellow with two kids is what you want then I suppose you know what you're doing.'

Nothing changes with James, she thought angrily, carping and criticising the moment he set eyes on her. 'Yes, as a matter of fact I *do* know what I'm doing,' she told him coldly, and if that wasn't the overstatement of the year her name wasn't Helen Blake.

'I see. I'll let you get on with your child-minding, then,' he said disdainfully, and strode off to join the girl waiting for him.

Up to the time of Thomas and Jonathan going to bed there had been no call from Daniel, and once they were asleep the house settled into a waiting silence, while Helen's restlessness increased. She was bursting to talk to him but the opportunity wasn't presenting itself. Bruno had said that he'd rung each evening to speak to the children and make sure that all was well, and she was expecting tonight to be the same, and when he came on the line he was in for a surprise. Whether he would find it a pleasant one she didn't know.

But the hours dragged by and the telephone was silent, and at last, miserable and on edge, she went to bed. Bruno had left details of an emergency number that Daniel could be reached on in Bangladesh, but she hadn't been able to bring herself to use it. There *was* a crisis at this end, but it was hers alone, and of her own making, and so she undressed, lay in his bed once more, and prayed he might ring before morning.

He didn't, and as they were eating breakfast Jonathan said, 'When's Daddy coming home, Helen? He's been away a long time.'

She managed to find a reassuring smile. 'Soon, Jonathan. I'm expecting him to call any moment to tell us when he'll be home, and in the meantime what shall we do today?'

It passed pleasantly enough, but as the sun set over the park Helen vowed that if he hadn't rung by midnight *she* was going to ring *him*, as now she had a feasible reason for doing so. He'd been in touch every other night, so why not last night? Maybe something was wrong, and she went cold at the thought, but she wasn't going to allow herself to dwell on the myriad awful things that could happen at home and abroad.

She watched the clock crawl through each hour and on the dot of twelve rang the number he'd left. It seemed an eternity before she got through, though in fact it must only have been seconds before a connection was made.

'Can I speak to Daniel Reed, please?' she asked quickly. There seemed to be some doubt at the other end as to who he was, and Helen explained, 'He's one of the paediatric surgeons from Britain who have been co-opted by Lars someone or other.'

That seemed to clarify matters and she listened carefully to the message at the other end. Mr Reed had left the previous morning and given instructions that if anyone should telephone regarding his whereabouts he was on his way home.

Relief washed over her. There was nothing wrong. Daniel was in transit, and if she could discover which flight he was on it would give some idea of when he would arrive home. But there was no passenger 'Reed' on any of yesterday's flights, or on today's, and alarm spiralled inside her again. Where was he?

By Wednesday evening Helen was frantic, as Daniel hadn't been recorded on any flight out of Bangladesh in the last three days, and to make matters worse Thomas hadn't eaten his tea and was saying that his throat hurt and he felt sick. With an urgent need for reassurance she found herself acting as the average parent would, and sent for a GP. . .in this instance her father.

He came as soon as evening surgery was over and when she opened the door to him he said jovially, 'And what's this, then? My doctor daughter sending for her old dad?'

Helen smiled weakly. 'Daniel should have been home two days ago and he hasn't arrived. I'm so apprehensive I can't think straight. I don't think I'm capable of making a diagnosis if there is one to be made.'

Her father smiled his comforting smile. 'Let's have a look at the little one, then.'

As they went up the stairs she said, 'I know it must seem as if I'm over-reacting, me of all people, but if anything happens to Daniel's children while they're in my care I wouldn't be able to face him again.'

'That's understandable,' he agreed, 'but there's the other side of the coin, you know.'

'What do you mean?'

'He's extremely fortunate to have someone like you to care for them. . .and him, because you do care for him, don't you?'

'Yes, I do,' she said sombrely, 'and the moment I see him again I'm going to tell him so, but at this moment Thomas is my main concern.'

'Could be the start of chicken-pox,' he said when he'd examined the feverish child. 'Temperature's up and glands tender. You're probably in for an uncomfortable twenty-four hours until the spots are out and then he'll feel a lot better.

'Don't forget that your mother and I are here for you

if you need us, and don't worry about Reed, he'll turn up.'

'But three days,' she said raggedly, 'almost four in fact. It doesn't take that long to come from Bangladesh.'

As the night wore on Thomas became more poorly and, when Helen checked, sure enough there were watery blisters behind his ears, in his mouth, and under his armpits. A couple of days should see him over the worst, but in the meantime he was a hot, fretful child who kept calling for his daddy.

Where are you, Daniel? Helen cried silently as she nursed him. Why aren't you here with us?

But her questions remained unanswered, and she knew if he hadn't appeared by morning she was going to contact the police. He could have been ambushed on the way to the airport, or be lying unidentified in a hospital somewhere. There had to be something strange going on, as she knew that Daniel would never normally leave his children for so long without a word.

Helen put Jonathan into Daniel's bed so that he wouldn't be disturbed, as she intended to spend the night in a chair beside Thomas. She changed into a nightdress and slipped a silk robe over it, removed her make-up, flicked a comb through her hair, and told herself that she was ready for the night ahead, while admitting that it was far more wearing caring for the sick when one was personally involved. Long stints on the wards and in Theatre were exhausting, but the impersonality of the situation carried one through. Here she had one sick little boy with a less than serious illness and she felt as if all the world was on her shoulders.

As dawn was breaking Thomas fell into a restful sleep for the first time, and when she saw that he was settled Helen went to the window where the first pink smudge of daybreak was brightening the night sky. The garden was shadowed and still, and in the house was the same waiting silence that had been there ever since that first night. If Daniel didn't turn up soon she would go insane, she thought wretchedly, as she turned away from the window, and, sinking back on to the chair, she closed her eyes and within seconds weariness triumphed; with her head on her arm, she slept.

She didn't hear the key turn in the lock, or the firm footsteps on the stairs, but when he spoke her name softly her hazel eyes flew open, and in that moment of supreme joy they filled with tears that overflowed on to her cheeks.

'Minnehaha! What are *you* doing here?' he asked in an amazed whisper.

'What does it look like?' she cried through her tears. 'I'm looking after Thomas and Jonathan. Bruno had to go back to Germany. . .and where have you been? I've been frantic. How *could* you just disappear without a word?'

He took her hands in his and pulled her gently to her feet. 'I'll tell you in a moment, but first, what's wrong with Thomas?'

'Chicken-pox,' she croaked. 'He started to be unwell yesterday and has had a bad night, but the rash is out now and he should soon be on the mend.'

Daniel smiled with relief. 'If that's all, we can cope, I think. He seems peaceful enough at the moment so shall we go downstairs and I'll tell you where I've been!'

Helen nodded mutely and followed him down the wide staircase, thinking as she did so that if ever there was an occasion when she wasn't looking her best this was it. Face blotched with weeping, hair awry, hands clenched on a sodden tissue. Why couldn't she have been awake and serenely beautiful when he came home?

He led the way into the sitting-room and as she perched uneasily on the edge of the couch she saw the fatigue in his face. He looked travel-weary and crumpled, and she took comfort in the knowledge that Daniel wasn't looking his best either.

His look was serious, a measuring sort of glance that increased her nervousness. Was he about to inform her that he'd spent the last few days in a cosy love-nest somewhere?

She would soon know. He was opening his mouth to speak. 'You will know by now where I've been, I presume, Helen,' he said quietly.

Helen bent her head. 'Yes, and I'm so ashamed of the way I behaved. . .'

He gave a tired grin. 'That's all right, forget it. I know you're a stickler for honour and I wouldn't have you any other way. I respect you for it.'

Respect! What a prim word, but then it described her exactly. She *was* prim, and, restraining the urge to start howling again, she fixed him with puffy eyes and said abjectly, 'There was no excuse for my jumping to wrong conclusions.'

'I've told you, it's all right, Helen,' he repeated, 'and now we've cleared that up I'm going to bring you up to date on my activities. I was persauded to go to Bangladesh by my friend Lars Olsen. I agreed to go for just the one week as I didn't want to be away from those I love any longer.'

Did that include herself? she wondered.

'However, it occurred to me during that week that as I'd already flown halfway across the world I might as well travel a bit further.'

Helen was staring at him blankly. 'You've been somewhere else? Where? What for?'

His straight blue gaze didn't falter. '*Yes*. . . I've been somewhere else. *Where*. . . Kashmir. *What for*. . .you'll probably think me crazy, but I've been to tell Kerwin that I love you,. . .and I think that you love me.'

'You've been to K2!' she gasped.

'To the foothills, yes. I hired a Jeep and drove as far as I could go in safety. I placed a wreath of mountain lily on the slopes which I thought would please you, and then I gave that huge pile of ice and snow my message for Kerwin.'

'You went to Kashmir because of me?' she said in an awed whisper.

'Because of *us*, my love,' he told her. 'I felt I had to make a gesture of some sort, as I don't want our marriage to be a threesome. I've said a farewell for you, Helen. Do you think you could begin to look forward now. . .and love *me* as much as you love my children?'

She sprang to her feet and gazed into his unforgettable face. 'I love you all equally, my darling,' she breathed. 'With the children it's a protective love because they're small and vulnerable — delightful — but my love for you is the most marvellous thing that's ever happened to me, and I can't believe you return it.

'You're asking me if I'm ready to look forward. I've been doing that from the moment you gazed up at me from this very spot, Daniel. Damp and bedraggled as I was that day, it didn't stop me from thinking that here was a man I wanted to see more of. . .and amazingly my wish was granted.

'I was wary of you at first because you were so different from Hugh Copley, and because I'd allowed myself to become so pedantic, but it didn't take me long

to realise that we had a lot in common.' Her voice
trembled. 'Especially after that night at the open-air
theatre.'

His smile was tender. 'So you haven't forgotten?'

The colour flared in her face. 'Of course not! I've
been consoling myself with the thought that I would
have at least that to remember if you didn't want
anything else to do with me after the way I behaved.'

Daniel held out his arms. 'Come here,' he commanded gently, and when she was encircled against the
broad comforting strength of him he told her huskily,
'Do you really think I would want to lose my beautiful,
adorable, prickly woman because of a small misunder-
standing? The woman who makes my blood race and
my heart leap with delight? Who gave up her free time
to care for my children, and is a fine and caring doctor?'

His eyes went over the face upturned to his, and he
saw the promise of all the joy to come in her eyes, and a
passion to match his own in the soft curve of her lips.
Tender laughter rumbled in his throat. 'No, I couldn't
bear to lose you, Helen. Danny Boy knows when he's
on to a good thing.'

And as his mouth caressed her throat, and his arms
held her even closer, now completely serious, he murmured softly, taking her back in time and yet surely
describing the present, '"As unto the bow the cord is,
So unto the man is woman; Though she bends him, she
obeys him, Though she draws him, yet she follows;
Useless each without the other."'

JANET
DAILEY

A Collection

Three sensuous love stories from a world-class
author, bound together in one beautiful volume—
A Collection offers a unique chance for new fans to
sample some of Janet Dailey's earlier works and for
longtime readers to collect an edition to treasure.

Featuring:

THE IVORY CANE
REILLY'S WOMAN
STRANGE BEDFELLOW

Available from May   Priced £4.99

W✹RLDWIDE

LOVE ON CALL
4 FREE BOOKS AND 2 FREE GIFTS
FROM MILLS & BOON

Capture all the drama and emotion of a hectic medical world when you accept 4 Love on Call romances PLUS a cuddly teddy bear and a mystery gift - absolutely FREE and without obligation. And, if you choose, go on to enjoy 4 exciting Love on Call romances every month for only £1.80 each! Be sure to return the coupon below today to: Mills & Boon Reader Service, FREEPOST, PO Box 236, Croydon, Surrey CR9 9EL.

--- **NO STAMP REQUIRED** ---

YES! Please rush me 4 FREE Love on Call books and 2 FREE gifts! Please also reserve me a Reader Service subscription, which means I can look forward to receiving 4 brand new Love on Call books for only £7.20 every month, postage and packing FREE. If I choose not to subscribe, I shall write to you within 10 days and still keep my FREE books and gifts. I may cancel or suspend my subscription at any time. I am over 18 years. Please write in BLOCK CAPITALS.

Ms/Mrs/Miss/Mr _____ **EP63D**

Address _____

_____

Postcode _____ Signature _____

mps
**MAILING
PREFERENCE
SERVICE**

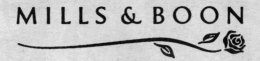

MILLS & BOON

HEARTS OF FIRE

By Miranda Lee

HEARTS OF FIRE by Miranda Lee is a totally compelling six-part saga set in Australia's glamorous but cut-throat world of gem dealing.

Discover the passion, scandal, sin and finally the hope that exists between two fabulously rich families. You'll be hooked from the very first page…

Each of the six novels in this series features a gripping romance. And the first title **SEDUCTION AND SACRIFICE** can be yours absolutely FREE! You can also reserve the remaining five novels in this exciting series from Reader Service, delivered to your door for £2.50 each. And remember postage and packing is FREE!

MILLS & BOON READER SERVICE, FREEPOST, P.O. BOX 236, CROYDON CR9 9EL. TEL: 061-684 2141

YES! Please send me my FREE book (part 1 in the Hearts of Fire series) and reserve me a subscription for the remaining 5 books in the series. I understand that you will send me one book each month and invoice me £2.50 each month.

NO STAMP NEEDED

MILLS & BOON READER SERVICE, FREEPOST, P.O. BOX 236, CROYDON CR9 9EL. TEL: 061-684 2141

EPHOF

Ms/Mrs/Miss/Mr: _____

Address _____

_____

_____

Postcode _____